70 Days of Pleasure

CHRISTINE PAULS

Silver Pen Publications, LLC

70 Days of Pleasure

CHRISTINE PAULS

♦ ACKNOWLEDGEMENTS ♦

Another literary accomplishment and I'm thankful. When I started my literary journey, I thought I'd be three books and done. But after becoming a member of NK Tribe Called Success, under the mentorship of Naleighna Kai, I have blossomed in ways I hadn't thought possible.

Thank you, Tribe. Your love and support uplifts me with every step I take. To beta readers, Kelsie Maxwell, and Deb Mitchell, thank you for your keen skillset and critique. It truly helped me to re-evaluate and see things from a reader's point of view. Also, thank you to Terri Ann Johnson, my sister scribe and Tribe member for her reading my manuscript and critiquing.

Participating in this series has given me a new lease on literary life.

Chapter 1

Huntsville, Texas

Fresh out of prison, Conway Ackerman sat, in a cheap, motel room, his piercing blue eyes vacant, staring at the images on the forty-two-inch, flatscreen television on the dresser occupied the space. A cigarette dangled from his lips, a long ash hanging by a thread.

A free man, only twenty-four hours ago, had a deadly plan whose mission was to seek out and destroy his incompetent, public defender, Allen Hicks, Judge Mallory and his prize possession, Dallas Avery. Five years at Huntsville Unit gave him plenty of time to plot their demise, and it was time to put his plan into action.

Conway raked his fingers through his greasy, blonde strands, then grabbed a beer off the nightstand. He drank the entire can of frothy liquid in one gulp, letting out a disgusting belch. An evil laugh bellowed from the bottom of his belly. Lying down on the uncomfortable bed, he crossed one leg over the other, closed his eyes, and drifted off to sleep.

* * *

Coalwood, West Virginia

The beating Elmer Ackerman inflicted on his son was brutal.

With blood-stained hands, he dragged the small frame into the living room, flinging his battered body in front of his mother.

"Clean him up," he ordered, then went into the kitchen to retrieve a beer from the refrigerator. On his way to the bedroom, the small body still claimed the space on the carpet where he left it. His eyes bore into Maggie Ackerman.

"Are you deaf? Didn't I say…" and with a closed fist, landed a punch that connected with her jaw.

Blood spewed from her mouth. She raised both hands to protect her face from any more of her husband's wrath. She cried, "I'm sorry, please no more."

"Then do what the hell I tell you. "He growled.

Maggie crawled to her son's broken body and dragged him to the bathroom.

The words expelled from Maggie's mouth. "You'll never amount to anything," she said cleaning the bloody wounds with alcohol to inflict more agony.

Conway cried a river from the debilitating sensation. Mommy, please. It hurts."

She slapped him across the face, leaving a rosy, handprint. "If you'd done what you were told, none of this would've happened to you or me. I hate the sight of your ugly ass."

Maggie snatched the burning cigarette from the ledge of the sink and inhaled deeply, causing her to cough.

"Go to your room," she said and pushed him towards the bathroom exit.

Each word felt like a dagger to his heart. Conway examined his reflection in the mirror, then trudged out of the bathroom, to his room, leaning on the wall for support. The pain was excruciating, as he tried to find a comfortable position on the dirty mattress, hate fueling the desire to see them both dead.

* * *

Conway opened his eyes. The vision of his parents' abuse, and neglect remained engraved in his mind. At the age of twelve, the house burned down, killing his parents, allegedly, due to his mother falling asleep with a cigarette in her hand. What remained was smoke, ashes, and the stench of death. The scene excited Conway, knowing he was to blame and the two people he despised the most were burning in hell.

The rest of his childhood days were spent in different foster homes, until he was eighteen, when the streets became his primary residence. Trouble followed him in and out of prison and his mental capacity continued to deteriorate. While incarcerated, the diagnosis of dissociative identity disorder was identified by a psychiatrist who took the time to care. The abuse inflicted upon Conway, caused him to create the alter ego which carried him through all the trauma he experienced.

He sat at the foot of his bed and marveled at the life size poster of his favorite basketball star, Dallas Avery. Conway advanced to the image and plastered his body against the glossy, twenty-four by thirty-six image. His tongue traveled over the face. Moaning with satisfaction, the release stained his briefs.

"This is going to be epic, Conway." The words sang from his throat.

"I don't want to do this, Julian." Conway shook his head.

"Of course, you do." The voice emanated throughout his brainwaves. *"And we will. I can't allow him to live after you've spent five years in prison, only trying to be his friend and he rejected you. He rejected us."*

"You overstepped your boundaries and I suffered for it. I am the one who spent those years in prison. Time served alone and you never once came to my aid." Conway held both hands over his head, trying to stop the pain.

"My, my, are we having a tantrum? I didn't come to keep you company because you were at fault. Now it's time for you to correct the mistake. Go ahead and have your fun with the others. They mean nothing to me. Find him! Understand?"

Christine Pauls

Chapter 2

Harris County Criminal Courts at Law, Houston, TX

Allen Hicks glanced over at the pile to his right and pulled a manila folder from the top. A public defender for seven years, he thought his legal career would be far more advanced, instead of being overworked, underpaid, and undervalued.

He pushed his bifocals up on his brown face and flipped through the file of his latest assigned case. Although innocent until proven guilty, the heavy workload made it hard to give proper representation to the guilty or innocent.

Allen sighed, rubbing his hand over his close-cut waves, as he put the remaining files in the cart by his side, and ambled to the vault. He pressed the four-digit combination on the keypad, then pushed open the metal door.

Allen removed the folders and placed them on the table to begin the task of filing the documents in alphabetical order, while humming his favorite Katie Perry song, *I Kissed a Girl*.

Making room to insert documents in the letter A, he pulled out Conway Ackerman's file.

"Good ole Conway," Allen smirked. "The worst of the worst."

He opened the file to see the red stamp that read, RELEASED on the front page. The gasp from his mouth caused him to drop the folder on the floor, papers scattering everywhere.

"When?" he said, fumbling through the papers. "Forty-eight hours ago?"

Allen bent down, picking up the files with shaking hands. The thought of this deranged person roaming the streets, would have anyone peeking over their shoulder…Especially him.

He rubbed his eyes, then gathered his belongings and made his way to the parking lot. Late nights were the norm. He waved goodnight to a sleeping security guard at the desk and took the stairs to the basement.
***

The door squeaked as it opened. Allen peeked out, looking from left to right. At ten at night, the lot was empty and mute. His brisk strides were met with footsteps behind him. Allen fumbled for the keys to his 1999, Mazda Protégé. His hands trembled as he unlocked the door, throwing everything on the passenger side seat. The stabbing pain in his side caused him to inhale a sharp breath.

Grabbing his jacket, Conway pulled Allen to him and whispered in his ear. "Hello, Allen." He pushed the knife blade deeper into his side.

Allen gasped from the unbearable pain. "Help me," he whispered.

"No one can hear you, Allen." Conway smirked. "I've waited five long years to see you again. Aren't you happy to see me?" Conway snatched the knife out of Allen's side then pushed him to the ground. His glasses breaking as he fell on his face.

Allen moaned in agony, his breathing shallow. "Conway, please," he whimpered. "I did the best I could. You know that. Please don't."

Conway knelt next to Allen. He flipped him over and placed his face inches away from the dying man. "You did your best? How can you say that? You didn't fight for me and sent an innocent man to prison. That, I can't forgive."

"But you weren't innocent...The deal..." Allen coughed up blood.

Conway plunged the knife deep into Allen's chest. He continued to stab him until blood sprayed over his face and clothing. The body convulsed, then stilled. Allen's eyes remained opened and fixed.

"Die, Allen." Conway wiped blood from his face with his hands. "Don't fight the inevitable."

He snatched the knife out of the lifeless body and wiped blood on the front of Allen's navy blue, blazer and rummaged through his pockets, retrieving his wallet.

Standing, Conway admired his handywork. "One down. Two to go." He stepped out into the night and slid in the driver's seat of a stolen, black Camry and sped off.

Chapter 3

Houston, Texas, 8:00 am

Dallas lurched forward in his chair, "What do you mean Conway Ackerman is out of prison? Has it been five years?"

"Yes, it has. I wouldn't worry about it, Dallas. What happened is all behind you now," Katie, his agent, said.

"When did he get out? Where is he?" Dallas rambled.

"About a week ago from what I'm told. All I'm aware is that he's a free man, but I'll try and find out. He doesn't have any family that we know of.. Maybe he went back to where he came from. Somewhere in West Virginia. Are you going to tell Alicia?"

Dallas tapped the tips of his fingers on the mahogany desk. "I don't know," he said. "It happened long before I met her. I don't want her to worry."

"Are you worried?" Katie quizzed.

Dallas swiveled his chair to face the scenery outside his window. He rubbed his chin. "He's a crazy, son-of-a-bitch, Katie. Maybe I'm thinking too much into this. Let's hope he went back to West Virginia."

"I believe you are making more of this than necessary. Besides, it's best that we know he's a free man, right?" Katie said in a matter-of-fact manner.

Dallas let out a long breath. "I guess. That bastard made my life a living hell. I don't want to have to deal with his bullshit again. Plus, Alicia…I don't want her involved. Then I'd have to kill him."

"You're talking like the man is coming after you." Katie paused. "Is that what you think?"

"I don't know what I think right now. I'll concern myself with Ackerman later."

"Sounds good to me," Katie chuckled. "We have more pressing matters at hand, like Nashville."

***

Out of the blue, Dallas said, "Come to Nashville with me." Then he continued eating a stack of French toast smothered in butter and warm syrup.

Putting her fork down on the marble countertop, Alicia glanced up. "What's in Nashville?

"I have an endorsement meeting, then I figured we could spend a few days and enjoy the sights and each other." Dallas gave a mischievous smile and winked.

"Sounds wonderful, but I can't stay with you forever, Dallas. You know that, right?"

Dallas frowned as he pondered the words that tumbled out of Alicia's mouth. He didn't speak, keeping his gaze on the woman who made him feel like nothing else mattered in his world but her. Why she would say such a thing was beyond him.

"You know I didn't mean it that way, honey. I can see that you're serious about Nashville, aren't you?" She asked, picking up her fork, cutting into a vegetable omelet.

Dallas smiled. "Are you saying, yes?"

Alicia gazed into his eyes. "Of course. I wouldn't say no unless it was necessary."

"Great," Dallas said. "Why don't you go pack while I make this call to Katie. She wants to discuss my itinerary and the details of the meeting with Philip Ardmore. We leave tomorrow. Thanks, baby." He kissed her, then did a two-step to his office.

Alicia's heart fluttered with anticipation. An impromptu meeting at a charity auction had turned into the most unexpected pleasure. She felt like she was in a dream that she didn't want to wake up from. Dallas made her happy. Although he was younger, a lot younger, they clicked on an even field of maturity. She hurried to pack her bags, wondering if she'd have to wake up from this fantasy at some point.

Chapter 4

Houston Executive Airport

The two entered the luxurious, private aircraft and settled back in the leather seats. Alicia closed her eyes and Dallas encased her hand in his.

"I hope you don't mind that I changed our method of travel to private, baby?" He asked, massaging the inside of her palm. "I didn't feel like all the attention from the media and the public as we maneuvered through the airport and on the plane."

"I'm fine with whatever you think is best. You know, I'm a little tired from last night." She grinned and placed her head on his shoulder, engrossed in the warmth of his touch.

"I'm sorry I can't keep my hands off you." He brushed the sides of her face with his hands.

She gazed into his eyes. "The feelings are mutual."

"Go ahead and take a power nap. We'll be in Nashville in about an hour and a half."

Alicia didn't argue. She kissed him and reclined her seat.

As she slept, Dallas covered her with a blanket and moved to another seat. He pulled out his cell and located his mother's number in his contact information. He wished he could share the news of meeting Alicia, but deep down he knew, now wasn't the time to drop what he knew would explode like Juneteenth fireworks. His mother would hardly be happy about him being with a woman almost twice his age. He paused, then pressed her number and waited.

"Son how are you," Anna greeted.

"I'm good Mom. How's everything?"

"Everything is fine," she said, the sound of sizzling oil in the background. "Where are you?

"On my way to Nashville for business, an endorsement opportunity. What are you cooking? I hear that oil popping."

"Frying up some chicken. I already made a little potato salad, and candied yams. Got some leftover collards I'm going to heat up. Will Katie be with you?"

"For sure, Mom. How's Pops?" Dallas changed the subject. He knew his mother wanted to dig deeper but hoped she wouldn't press for any more information right now. He didn't lie to her or keep secrets. This was difficult not to be completely honest.

"He's all right. In the family room watching TV," Anna said, flatly.

Dallas sensed a shift in his mother's demeanor. He knew that his father wasn't the easiest man to live with. Dealing with the man hadn't been easy for him lately either. They always seemed to be at odds, and it put a strain on their relationship.

"Y'all good?" Dallas asked in a more serious tone.

"As well as can be expected, Son." Anna answered nonchalantly.

"What does that mean. Is there a problem?" Dallas pressed.

"Nothing, son. Everything is fine. It's only the truth, as you well know."

"You're right, Mom. It's just that I want you to tell me if it's not, that's all. Anyway, have you spoke to Carrie? Is everything okay with her?"

"First, I would tell you if it was something, I felt you needed to know when it comes to the relationship between your father and me. However, I'm the mother and you're the son. Let me deal with him. As far as your sister, well, if something was going on, she wouldn't tell me because she doesn't want me to speak out of turn about her husband, but I ask anyway and don't have a choice but to take her word. The thing is, if you're not going to leave the marriage, there's no sense of complaining when existing problems arise. You understand?"

"Yeah. I understand what you're saying." Dallas agreed.

The conversation went on for another twenty minutes. If anyone understood him, his mother did. Her calm demeanor kept him grounded and her support of his dreams allowed him to pursue and bring them to fruition.

"I'll come through when I get back. You know how to reach me."

"I do and I won't. See you when you get home. I love you."

"Love you, too." Dallas chuckled.

After disconnecting the call, Dallas moved back to his seat next to a still sleeping Alicia. He watched the rise and fall of her chest and the cleavage from the perfectly fitted, fuchsia, knit top that molded her breasts perfectly. Alicia Mitchell was the most beautiful creation. He reclined and relaxed his body back into the soft, leather seat and closed his eyes, still feeling uneasy.

Chapter 5

The Heights, Houston TX, 6:30 pm

"John, over here." Melvin waved.

Every Thursday, the two Black judges, met at The Heights, a cigar lounge, fifteen minutes away from the Harris County Criminal Courts of Law, to relax, chat and enjoy the smooth, nutty flavor of a cylinder rolled in Nicaraguan tobacco leaves.

John nodded and moved through the room, the gray suit fitting his six-foot one frame, meeting Melvin at a round, cherry wood, table with two, vintage leather club chairs. Both men shook hands, then embraced.

"What's good, man?" Melvin sat down and crossed one leg over the other. His bald head shined and his salt and pepper, neatly cut beard glistened in the light. "I took the liberty of ordering these." He pointed to four Juan Lopez cigars, "and Courvoisier to wash it down." He chuckled.

"I've been thinking about a good cigar all day, my man. How's the family?" John reached for a cigar.

"Everyone is well. My wife is planning a trip to Belize for our twenty-fifth anniversary. I'm looking forward to getting away and enjoying my spouse and downtime. And you?"

"All is well on my end, but from a work perspective, I found out some disturbing news." John cut the tip and lit his cigar. He puffed, then blew the smoke out of his nose.

Melvin frowned, leaning forward in his chair. "What's going on?"

Before John could answer, the server returned with two goblets of cognac and placed them on the table in front of them. "Will there be anything else?" she asked.

"No, we're good for now," Melvin said. The server nodded and moved to another table.

John picked up his cognac and took a few sips. "Conway Ackerman is out of prison. Five years has come and gone."

"Why are you bothered? He deserved more time, if you ask me, for stalking Dallas Avery."

"I know," John said, "But when you come across a person whose mental capacity is less than stellar and feels no remorse for what they've done, a person like that, should never be able to walk the streets free."

"You don't think he would seek revenge, do you?" Melvin puffed his cigar, then exhaled.

John sipped the last remnants of his cognac. "You can never be sure. I remember the menacing glare he gave me as he was being led out of the courtroom. I'll never forget it."

Melvin gave John's shoulder a squeeze. "Drink and enjoy the cigar, my friend. The last thing you need to be thinking about is Conway Ackerman."

"You're right." John relaxed in his chair, with the thought of Conway Ackerman in the back of his mind.

The two men enjoyed the rest of the evening talking about work, family, and current events. Before they knew it, two hours had passed.

"Well, man," Melvin sipped the last of his cognac. "Guess we better get home to our families." Melvin removed his jacket that was draped on the back of the chair and slipped it on.

"I agree. I look forward to Thursdays. Same time, same place next week?' John put on his jacket and they both headed to the exit.

"You know it," Melvin said.

Outside, both men said their goodnights and parted ways.

***

John strolled down the block, to his car. Removing the keys from his inside jacket pocket, he pressed the fob to disarm the alarm on the midnight blue, BMW 5 Series. As he walked to the driver's side to get in, he glanced up to see a car barreling down the street towards him.

Before John could react, the car hit him, head on, sending his body airborne, smashing through a storefront window. People screamed and ran to and away from the gruesome sight.

Melvin ran towards the commotion. He saw John's damaged car and people gathered in front of a building. "John," he yelled. Melvin pushed through the crowd and saw his friend, dead. He fell to his knees and wept. "Oh my God, no."

At the end of the block, the damaged front end, of an older model black Camry, sat idling, then turned the corner. Conway pulled into a vacant lot, slid out of the car. "Two down. One to go."

***

After his mini killing spree, Conway returned to his motel room. He pulled out his phone and Googled, Dallas Avery. There was an article about the basketball icon, coming to Nashville to meet with Ardmore Sports regarding an endorsement opportunity.

Conway focused on the story until the idea hit him like a bolt of lightning.

"Nashville," he yelled. Digging in is jean pocket he pulled out the wallet of his latest

victim and rummaged through, finding a few hundred dollars in cash.

"Thanks, Allen," he chuckled. "Nashville here I come." He'd find Dallas Avery, come hell or highwater.

Chapter 6

Nashville, Tennessee, 10:30 am

"We're here." Dallas gently touched Alicia's shoulder. Her eyes fluttered opened.

"I feel like I just fell asleep." Alicia yawned and stretched.

Even when she did something as simple as stretching her body, it turned him on. "When we get to the hotel, you can crash for a while," he said, giving her hand a gentle squeeze.

"Sounds good. I need a little more sleep," Alicia said, moving in closer.

"It's my fault and I'm sorry." Dallas kissed her cheek.

"It's not all your fault." She winked.

Exiting the plane, they were led to a private exit where a black, town car awaited them.

* * *

The car pulled up in front of the iconic and luxurious, Hermitage, located in downtown Nashville. The outside of the structure was designed in an architectural style called Beaux-Arts which combined classical architecture from ancient Greece and Rome with Renaissance ideas.

Entering the hotel, hands locked together, both jaws dropped. The grand staircase, marble floors, columns, and ornate chandeliers were spectacular. But what caught their eye the most, was the painted glass skylight. The multi colors gave off brilliant rays.

"This is the most beautiful sight," Alicia said. "I can't believe we are staying here." Her eyes wandered, capturing its beauty.

"Yes, it is and yes we are," Dallas said. "I thought the photos were nice, but seeing it live and in living color, they hardly do it justice. I read that this hotel has been around since 1910 and was a favorite among celebrities and politicians like JFK and Johnny Cash. Thought it'd be nice to stay here and leave our mark." He winked and gave her a sly grin.

"Our mark, indeed." Alicia beamed, unable to resist his charm.

"Let's get checked in and we can go from there."

"Okay," Alicia said, still admiring the grand hotel.

"This way, Mr. Avery. It's all taken care of." The manager motioned.

Dallas nodded. "Cool, thanks, man. This way, baby." He placed his hand at the small of her back and led her to an elevator located behind a set of elegantly carved, ebony wood, double doors.

"Well look at this 007 stuff right here. You wouldn't know this was an elevator." Alicia ran her fingers through the lines of the curves of wood.

"That part." Dallas laughed. "Secret agent stuff right here."

"Mr. Avery." A young man quickly pushing a luggage rack, approached them.

"Welcome to the Hermitage. My name is Albert, and I will be your attendant and if I may say, I'm a huge fan." He rambled, extending his hand and Dallas gave him a firm handshake.

"Nice to meet you, Albert, and thank you. This is, Ms. Mitchell."

"Pleasure to meet you, ma'am." Albert nodded.

Alicia glanced in Dallas's direction, giving him a look.

"Good to meet you, Albert," she said.

"Allow me to escort you to your room. I can imagine you're fatigued from travel."

"Yes, we could use some rest. Lead the way, Albert," Dallas motioned with his hand.

The elevator doors opened, and they stepped inside.

* * *

Arriving at the Presidential Suite, Albert removed the key card from his jacket pocket, and inserted the white object into the slot, pushed the door open, and then handed it to Dallas. As they started to enter, Albert held his hand up in a stopping motion. "Just a moment," he said and disappeared into the suite.

Returning, Albert said, "I wanted to make sure everything was as it should be. Follow me," he said, pushing the luggage rack inside, followed Dallas and Alicia inside the suite.

"Is there anything else I can get for you?"

"No, Albert. The suite meets all of our expectations." Dallas reached into his pocket and pulled out two crisp one-hundred-dollar bills.

"Here you go, Albert. Thank you."

Albert's eyes widened at the sight of the monetary blessing.

"Thank you so much, Mr. Avery. I really appreciate this."

Dallas patted him on the back. "You're welcome and call me Dallas."

"All right, thank you, Dallas. Enjoy your stay. Please call if you need anything."

"We will." Dallas waved and shut the door.

"He's a nice, young man," Alicia said, putting her purse on the bed, then stepping to the window to admire the view.

Dallas joined her and wrapped his arm around her waist. He said,

"I like him, too. He's a cool kid."

* * *

The suite was striking. Fifteen hundred square feet of the finest quality, plush furnishings, king-size bedroom, formal living area, marble bathroom, and powder room, butler's pantry, and a custom made, oval dining table. The breathtaking Nashville view was visible through a large window which would be a romantic backdrop at night. A baby blue, chaise was tucked by the window and the cobalt, with white stripe sofa and loveseat, dominated the space, along with a glass coffee table. Over the cherry wood mantle that showcased a wood-burning fireplace, hung a sixty-five-inch flat-screen TV.

Alicia sat on the bed after taking a tour of every inch of what would be their living space. She continued to admire its beauty until her attention went to Dallas who was watching her intensely.

"Are you happy?" He asked. "It's important to me that you are."

"Other than being called, ma'am, yes, I'm incredibly happy." Alicia kicked off her flats, and lay across the bed, closing her eyes. Its plushness engulfed her entire being.

"You're tired." Dallas lay next to her, pulling her close.

"This bed is telling me so and I'm going to give in."

"Why don't we get comfortable and take a nap." He grinned.

Alicia snickered. "I hope that's what happens, but I'm sure you'll make it very difficult."

"That's not my intention," he said in a playful tone. "You're irresistible, woman, and as much as I try, I can't keep my hands off you." Dallas rubbed his strong hands down the curves of her frame.

Alicia turned to face him and planted a gentle kiss on his lips which he welcomed.

"So much for napping," Dallas whispered in her ear.

Chapter 1

The Hermitage Hotel

Instead of getting some much-needed rest after an intense lovemaking session, Dallas lay, staring at the ceiling. The news of Conway Ackerman being out of prison, disturbed him a great deal. The man had caused many sleepless nights, over the four months he stalked his entire life. It was a nightmare, to say the least. Dallas thought this disturbed human had become a distant memory. Until now.

He turned to find his place near her and snuggled into the lines of her voluptuous curves. Alicia stirred but didn't wake from her peaceful state of slumber. Her beauty was enchanting even while sleeping. He ran his hand down the side of her face. "Wake up, sleepyhead." Dallas kissed her earlobe, moving down the nape of her neck. Alicia moaned.

"I can't do another round yet. I need more sleep." Her body wiggled against his manhood."

"Well, you're going to have to stop doing that."

"What?" she giggled.

"Are you hungry?"

"Famished." Alicia rubbed her stomach.

"Let's get up and order something to eat. Nothing extravagant. Here's the menu for the Capital Grille located in the hotel lobby," Dallas said after rummaging through the nightstand drawer. Tell me what you'd like, and I'll call and place the order. I'll get Albert to deliver it to our room."

Alicia stood, wrapping the satin sheet around her naked body. Scanning the menu, she said, "I'll have the half turkey club, no bacon, and a bowl of the tomato basil soup. I'm going to take a shower." She stood, giving a glance over her shoulder, and smiled as she allowed the sheet to drop to the floor.

Dallas' lips curved into a mischievous grin. "Give me a minute and I'll be right in."

Alicia winked and hurried into the bathroom.

When he heard the shower, Dallas removed his cell from his pocket. He'd turn it off because the constant vibration annoyed him. Pressing the power button, the device lit up like a Christmas tree. Texts from his agent confirming the endorsement meeting time, his mother wanting to make sure he made it to Nashville safely, and several missed calls from an unknown number with no voice message left. Something didn't feel right in his world right now.

***

The food arrived, piping hot. Dallas arranged the meals casually around the table. Alicia entered the space in a red, satin robe that brushed her thighs. The scent of Vera Wang Princess engulfed the room. Dallas rounded the table to her side and extended his hand, leading her to the seat beside him. He inhaled the fragrance, placing a kiss on her cheek.

"This looks yummy," Alicia eyed the spread before her. Dallas intertwined his hand in hers and they bowed their heads. "Lord, we thank you for this food. Bless the hands that prepared it and let it be nourishment for our bodies, Amen."

They both lifted their heads at the same time and their gazes locked momentarily.

"Amen." Alicia picked up her sandwich and took a bite. She noticed Dallas hadn't touched his burger.

"Are you all right?" She asked with concern.

"I'm cool." He lied. "Katie has been texting and emailing me all-day about the meeting tomorrow. She won't give me a minute's rest."

"Katie's only doing her job. A job she does very well. You'll be great, honey. Go ahead and dig into that burger." Alicia eyed the large, slightly pink piece of red meat, dripping with cheddar cheese.

"Want a taste?" Dallas put the burger close to her mouth and licked his lips.

"No thanks." Alicia put her hand up. "You know I don't eat red meat." She laughed. "You go right ahead and enjoy yourself. I honestly don't see where you put all that food. Fries and onion rings, Dallas?" She shook her head.

"You don't know what you're missing." Dallas bit into the juicy burger, cheese oozing down the sides. He closed his eyes as he chewed. "This is scrumptious. Don't worry, baby, I'll be able to work it off." He winked.

"I'm sure you will." Alicia shook her head and continued to enjoy her meal.

"I planned an outing for us after we eat. I think you'll enjoy it. Plus, it will help us work off the extra calories." Dallas said taking a sip of his iced tea.

"Oh?" Alicia's brow raised. "What did you plan?"

"Now why would I tell you? You'll find out soon enough."

Alicia put down her spoon and relaxed her back into the cushioned chair. She folded her arms over her ample breasts. "As you wish, my love. I'll be patient."

Dallas smiled and put his attention back on his meal. He knew this situation couldn't be kept from Alicia, and although this happened early in his career, before they knew of each other's existence, he couldn't keep her in the dark.

***

Conway Ackerman arrived, by Greyhound, in Nashville twenty-four hours later and checked into a Motel 6. He pulled out his phone, and using the motel's wi-fi, he put Dallas' name in the search, and saw a pic posted by the media of him stepping out of a black, town car and being escorted into The Hermitage Hotel in Nashville.

The unfortunate part was that the basketball icon wasn't alone. His plus one would be collateral damage. Reaching inside his top pocket he removed a cigarette from a box of Winston's, lit the narrow cylinder and put it in his mouth. He inhaled, then released ringlets of smoke in the air. The main event would take place at the swanky hotel when the time came to make his move.

* * *

Harris County Court at Laws, 2016

The jury foreman handed Judge Mallory a square piece of notepaper. He unfolded the square, sheet and glanced at the words, then placed it face down in front of him.

He turned to the jury, and asked, "So, say you all?"

The foreman nodded. "Yes, your Honor."

Judge Mallory motioned in the direction of the defense table. "Please stand, Mr. Ackerman."

Conway and his public defender, Allen Hicks stood. His body twitched as his alter-ego tried to take center stage. He fought the urge, keeping Julian at bay. The situation was already grim. No need to add more fuel into the equation.

"The jury finds you guilty of aggravated stalking and sentences you to five years which you will serve consecutively at Huntsville Unit. You will also undergo psychiatric evaluations over that time. This Court is adjourned."

Judge Mallory slammed the gavel on the podium, and Conway was taken away in handcuffs and chains.

Conway scanned the court room until his eyes connected with Dallas Avery. He grinned and mouthed, "See you soon, my friend."

The memory caused Conway's demeanor to harden. He covered his face with his hands as his alter ego's voice traveled through his psyche, causing pain as he stood behind a brick structure. Peering through a pair of binoculars he waited for the couple to arrive at the United Tour location on 4th Avenue. Another gem he'd found out about on the internet with their whereabouts.

The black town car pulled up on Fourth Avenue. The door opened, and Dallas and Alicia emerged. Cameras flashed as the couple made their way to the location. Seeing the couple, especially Dallas, made his blood boil. The man's demise couldn't come fast enough.

Chapter 8

Nashville, Tennessee

"Good afternoon, Mr. Avery and Ms. Mitchell. Welcome to United Tours. My name is Yolanda Neal and I'll be your guide. This three-hour tour is part walking and the other in a private vehicle which will make a series of pointed interest stops. We'll start with a one and a half mile walk downtown, where I'll be describing, and speaking on the past, present, and future, as well as popular neighborhoods along the way.

We'll then dive into the Civil Rights Movement. You'll experience the civil rights story, for example, Woolworth's that was located on 5th. It was the first sit-in at the lunch counter in 1960, when Nashvillians lived in segregation.

The next leg will focus on African American culture which dates back to 1779. Some of the stories I'll highlight on the tour will be, a slave who lived near Public Square and purchased freedom for her son. A black man who started his career as a janitor in a law office and became a lawyer. The free black woman who opened a sweets shop in the 1800s. There is so much black history in Nashville. When we complete this tour, you both will be amazed. Shall we get started?"

"Please," Alicia and Dallas answered in unison, locking hands together.

"Very good. This way, please." Yolanda motioned.

The walk started and Yolanda, pointed out sites until they came upon Woolworth's on 5th. Alicia and Dallas were filled with excitement to step inside history.

"In 1960, a group of young, black students from Fisk and Tennessee State universities, entered this establishment, dressed in collared shirts, heavy dress coats, and ties. When they entered, people became uncomfortable, and White store clerks claimed spots at the counter to prevent the black students from taking a seat. Employees scrambled to put up hand-written signs, but the students didn't disperse, and this would evoke the first sit-in during the 1960's civil rights movements."

"Powerful," Dallas said.

Alicia ran her hands over the photo of the black faces who fought for change. Dallas did the same. Both were enthralled so far in a tour that just started.

As they walked in the heart of downtown Nashville, it was incredible to see the history of Nashville from the African American viewpoint.

"What about the history of sports for our people?" Dallas asked.

"Blacks have paved the way in all areas of the sports arena," Yolanda said.

"What about here in Nashville?" Dallas continued to grill.

Yolanda nodded. "How could I forget?" She smiled. "Come with me and let's take a moment to discuss." She led them to a benched area and continued.

"Lester McClain was the first African American to play football at the University of Tennessee. He was drafted by the Chicago Bears but was released from the team prior to the season.

In all, African Americans continue to fight for the culture in society at large. Sports was no different." She paused, then continued. "They fought for change and earned championship and statistical excellence. Also, carved out new pathways in society, crossing the color barriers for change. Basketball, for example, since we have a star here.

Although outside of Nashville, Bill Russell, the most prolific winner in professional sports history captured an NBA championship in eleven of his thirteen seasons. Chuck Cooper, Earl Lloyd, and Nat Clifton broke the NBA color barrier.

"Now that's what I'm talking about," Dallas exclaimed. "Had it not been for athletes such as these, I wouldn't be here today."

"Facts," Alicia said, admiring Dallas proudly.

"In all, "Yolanda said, "Nashville sparked a nonviolent challenge to racial segregation in the city and across the South. In fact, Nashville's Civil Rights Movement was in constant flow, from desegregating public schools to lunch counter sit-ins as we saw in Woolworth's.

The day continued to be filled with wonder and a wealth of information. They visited the Civil Rights Room at the Nashville Public Library, Fisk University, and Hadley Park.

I'm happy to have had the honor to be your tour guide today, Dallas and Alicia. To be picked from many, I realized that I've made strides in accurate information and professionalism"

"I was told you were the best, and that's why I chose you." Dallas gave her a warm embrace. Alicia did the same. "Thank you for today. It was amazing."

"I agree. This was an awesome day. I couldn't ask for anything more when it comes to the history of our culture."

"I'm glad you enjoyed yourself, babe. I loved it too. It wore me out and I'm ready to kick back, order room service, and relax for tonight. Unless you want to do something?"

"No babe, I'm tired It was a full day. I'm with you; let's relax tonight."

Dallas reclined in the black, leather seat. Alicia positioned her body next to him, her head on his shoulder. Oscar glanced in the rear-view mirror and smiled at the lovebirds.

"Are we all set to head back to the hotel, Mr. Avery?"

"We're ready, Oscar," Dallas said, wrapping Alicia in his arms.

Oscar lifted the tinted, privacy window and turned on a smooth jazz station for the couple to enjoy, and slowly pulled off into the night.

* * *

Oscar alerted Dallas via text that they had arrived back at the Hermitage. The vibration startled Dallas, and his eyes opened wide, then traveled to the vision of loveliness beside him. He kissed her forehead gently.

"We're back, sweetheart," he whispered. "Let's get some rest."

Although her eyes were closed, Alicia's dreamy smile told Dallas she heard him. While she stretched, Dallas took in every movement of her frame.

"I loved everything about today. Thank you, baby. You did good."

Dallas smiled. "I'm glad you enjoyed yourself, as much as I did. The shower is calling me and I'm ready to get fresh and relax. What about you?"

She gazed into his eyes. "I'm ready to get comfortable with you."

"Sounds like a plan. We can chill and watch a movie or make our own movie." Dallas grinned, taking her hand in his. "Lead the way," Alicia said.

Chapter 9

Nashville, Tennessee

Alicia relaxed on the baby blue chaise near the window, admiring the view as she waited for Dallas to escort her to another surprise. The weather for the evening would be pleasant, with a slight chill, and Dallas asked her to dress comfortably so she put on a pair of Michael Kors, blue jeans, a gray, knit lightweight sweater, black leather jacket, and a pair of black, wingtip oxfords. They had a wonderful time the day before on the Black History tour. The experience, no matter how difficult made them even more proud to be in the skin they were in.

She reminisced about the night they shared. This time, they didn't make love physically but spent the entire night in each other's arms talking about any and everything. It was an intimacy she couldn't describe, nor had ever experienced. The way he caressed her, kissed her gently while she listened to every beat of his heart was nothing short of amazing. Dallas Avery made her feel whole, alive, and wanted.

"Baby," he called. "You ready?" Dallas entered the room looking as handsome as ever in a black, Gucci tracksuit, and a pair of custom-made black Air Jordan's with red soles.

"Wow, you wear the hell out of a pair of jeans." He walked up behind her, his hands following the curves of her hips and buttocks.

"Thank you. You're looking pretty dapper yourself." Alicia's body grew warm. It happened every time he touched her.

"Thanks. I do have one thing I have to do before we leave, though." He released his hold, turning her to face him.

"What's that? Her tone curious.

"Blindfold you." He removed a black mask from his jacket pocket.

Alicia gave him a side-eye and asked, "Why, Dallas?

"You'll see. It's a surprise, remember?" He wrapped her in his arms, planting a kiss on her forehead.

"Maybe a hint?" She whined.

"Nope." He shook his head. "Relax and trust me."

"Okay. You know I trust you." Alicia turned, awaiting the black mask to cover her eyes.

***

The town car came to a stop. Oscar exited and came around to the passenger side and opened the door. Dallas stepped out onto the runway.

"Come on, baby. Take my hand," Dallas said. Alicia reached for Dallas's hand, and he guided her out of the vehicle. She held tightly to his arm.

"I'm going to remove your blindfold now." He released her hold and stood behind her and held the mask on each side.

"Okay." Alicia's nervous energy kicked in.

Dallas let the black mask fall and she let out a gasp.

"Oh my God, Dallas. A plane?" Alicia covered her mouth. "Where are we going?"

"We are heading to Beale Street in Memphis. Are you ready to get this party started?"

"More than ready, baby. Let's get it." Alicia did a two-step on her way to the plane.

"Mr. Avery." My name is Captain Orlando Ferguson, your pilot and this is Monique Ortiz, your attendant. He extended his hand, giving a firm handshake.

"Nice to meet you both. This is my lady, Alicia Mitchell."

"Hello." Alicia smiled and nodded.

The flight should take approximately forty to forty-five minutes. Once we get you all settled, we'll prepare for takeoff."

"Sounds good," Dallas said, leading Alicia inside the plane.

"So plush." Alicia surveyed her surroundings. She chose a window seat and Dallas slid in beside her, planting a kiss on her lips. "I'll always make you happy, baby. I love you."

Alicia gazed into his eyes, touching his face. She studied him closely. "What's going on, Dallas? I know something is bothering you. Tell me."

Dallas closed his eyes, then opened them. He pressed his forehead against her. "I promise I will tell you, but not now."

Alicia frowned. "Dallas, please."

Dallas kissed her. "Later, baby. Let's relish tonight."

Alicia gave him a questioning stare. "All right, but I don't see how we're going to relish anything with unfinished business."

Chapter 10

Memphis, Tennessee

Beale Street was intoxicating. Dallas and Alicia strolled in and out of establishments, enjoying the sights and sounds.

"Karaoke." Dallas pointed to a place called Alfred's. "You game?"

Alicia stopped in her tracks, putting her hand on her hips. She said, "Do you think we should? You could draw a lot of attention and not in a good way."

"We'll be good. Security is close by. Besides, folks are probably too tipsy to notice," Dallas chuckled.

Alicia hesitated, then said, "I don't know how I feel about this Dallas. I don't want us to encounter any problems."

"Come on, baby, we'll be fine." He pulled her in the direction of the establishment. Against Alicia's better judgement, security or not, they went inside.

Sitting towards the back and Dallas put on his cap. It was entertaining to watch people attempt to sing and pretend they were stars. After a few folks delivered their renditions, the host asked if anyone else wanted to give it a go.

A man yelled. "Right here, I'd like to give it a shot."

He rose from his seat and walked to the stage. Dallas watched him move which was familiar, but it couldn't be him. His hair was dark brown, not blonde, and he was heavier than Conway Ackerman. The man didn't resemble him either. When he turned to face the audience, he was wearing sunglasses.

"Why is he wearing sunglasses?" Alicia asked.

"Maybe he's blind," Dallas chuckled.

Alicia looked at Dallas, noticing his demeanor had changed. "Do you want to leave?"

"No, I'm good. Let see what he's got, plus I want to participate."

Alicia's eyes grew wide. "Dallas, you can't be serious. Why do you want to draw attention to yourself? To us?"

"Baby, come on. Loosen up and have some fun."

* * *

On the stage, the man didn't speak, but only pointed to the song, and the music played, and belted out the lyric to Pharrell Williams' song *Happy*. He twirled around the stage, bursting into laughter. It got to a point where he had to be removed because his performance was too long and drawn out. Dallas was fixated on the man, in a peculiar way.

Alicia's eyes roamed from the man on stage, back to Dallas. "Let's go. We need to talk."

"I want to do some karaoke first." He got the attention of the host, who said, "We have someone else who'd like to give it a try.

They moved to the stage. Dallas requested Ain't to Proud to Beg by the Temptations. Alicia began to dance to the beat, watching the crowd, praying this wouldn't become a fiasco, and Dallas belted out the lyrics to the song. She couldn't help but do a double take because he didn't sound bad. She chimed in and the audience stood and joined in. It seemed no one reacted to the celebrity in the house.

"You went old school on a sister," Alicia said as they walked hand in hand down the block.

"Growing up, my mother played a lot of music. We were always surrounded by The Temptations, The Supremes, Marvin Gaye and more. I may be young, but it's in my blood and I love it as much as current day."

"I hear you. I love old school music. If you listen closely, there's a story being told, a lesson to be learned. Reminds me of happier times." Alicia reminisced.

"For sure. Crooners like Luther. His music lives on." Dallas twirled Alicia around and back, both laughing and absorbed in the moment, until Alicia stopped in her tracks. "Wait a minute. You're supposed to tell me what's going on. Stop playing with me, now."

Dallas turned her to face him. "Okay, I'm sorry. Let's go in here." He pointed to B. B. King's Blues Café. "I want you to meet somebody."

* * *

Inside was brightly decorated and paid homage to the great guitarist and those who paved the way in the Blues genre were showcased in black and white photos in the lobby area.

"You must be short-staffed if you're at the door." Dallas spoke to the man standing behind the podium. The two men embraced.

"I don't know about short-staffed, but a little bird told me they saw this famous basketball player cutting up at Karaoke Night in Alfred's with a beautiful woman," he said, his eyes darting between him and the woman at his side. "And your lady friend is?"

Alicia blushed and Dallas grinned. "Sorry," he chuckled. "Mr. Marvin this is Alicia Mitchell." Marvin gave her a quick once-over. He noticed the mature woman was exceptionally beautiful.

Alicia stepped forward and extended her hand. She said, "It's a pleasure to meet you."

Giving her hand a firm handshake in return, Marvin raised is eyebrow. "All formal, huh? I'd prefer a hug and call me Marvin if it's okay with you?"

"Certainly." Alicia stepped into his embrace and gave a warm hug.

"That's more like it." Marvin smiled, then turned his attention to Dallas.

"How's your mother and the family doing?"

"They're well, thanks."

Alicia observed the interaction and wondered who the jovial and handsome man was to Dallas. He was older, with smooth brown skin and glistening white hair that was close-cut and an evenly shaped beard. The man was fine. Dallas glanced at Alicia and cleared his throat.

"Alicia, Mr. Marvin coached me for two years in high school."

"That's right," Marvin said. "Now he's all famous and I couldn't be prouder because I knew he'd be a star. Now, look at him all grown up with a pretty lady to boot." He laughed. "Dallas is good people so you must be too."

"So, how long y'all been together?" Marvin asked, his eyes darting from Dallas to Alicia. "I haven't heard anything in the media or otherwise about you having a wife or a girlfriend. I know that I would've heard about that before you even got here."

Dallas' tone was serious when he said, "You won't see or hear about it, and I'd like to keep it that way, Mr. Marvin."

Marvin's eyes widened as he absorbed the words. "Oh sure, sure," he said. "I understand."

"Thanks. Would you happen to have a table for us?"

"There's a booth close to the stage. Follow me."

Chapter 11

More autographed photos lined the wall inside, and the music was electric. People whispered as Marvin and security moved them through the crowd. Dallas kept a protective hold on Alicia until they arrived at the booth. Alicia slid in, and Dallas sat next to her instead of across. He kissed her lips.

"Isn't this great?" Dallas scanned the crowded room. People were engrossed in conversations at the bar. Others were on the dance floor, swaying to the music from the live band on stage and the aroma of barbeque tickled his nostrils.

"I'm listening," Alicia said, getting straight to the point.

"All right, baby," Dallas said. "Can we order a drink first? You're going to need it."

"Okay," Alicia said, her tone hesitant.

Dallas flagged down the server, and a man quickly approached their table.

"Good evening, my name is Morgan." He placed, menus, silverware, napkins, two bottles of Voss water, and glasses of ice in front of them. "Welcome to B.B. King's. I'll be taking care of you this evening. He removed his pad and pen from his jacket pocket. "Can I get you something from the bar?"

"I'll have a glass of your best chardonnay, please," Alicia said, picking up the menu.

"I'll have Remy Martin on the rocks, thanks, Morgan."

"Very good." Morgan nodded. "I'll get your drinks and give you a chance to review the menu," he said, then disappeared into the crowd.

"All right." Alicia put the menu down and turned to face him. "Tell me what's going on."

Dallas rubbed his palms together, then took her hands in his. He said, "I found out today, Conway Ackerman was released from prison."

"Who is Conway Ackerman?" Alicia asked. "Am I supposed to know who this person is?"

Dallas exhaled a breath. "Earlier in my career, before I met you, this guy started stalking me. It escalated to the point of being excessive and dangerous. His mental state was not stable. I couldn't understand why he was obsessed with me, and at first, I didn't take it seriously until he started stalking me, showing up everywhere. He also attempted to break in my home and cause harm to me. He was arrested, convicted of aggravated stalking, and sentenced to five years."

"When did you find out that he'd been released?"

"Before we came here. Katie called and told me."

Alicia frowned. "And you didn't think I should know about this before now?"

"I'm sorry, baby. I didn't want you to worry."

Alicia didn't speak for a moment, then she asked, "So, you think he'll come after you again now that he's out?"

The conversation was cut short when Morgan returned. "Your drinks," he said, placing them down on the table in front of each of them. "Do you need more time to view the menu? I could make a few suggestions?"

"Please," Dallas said.

"Our most popular item would be The Lip-Smackin' ribs. Slow-cooked, fall off the bone pork ribs, seasoned with our spice rub blend, finished on the grill. Served with baked beans and coleslaw. Now if you don't eat pork, one of my personal favorites is the Bayou Shrimp and Grits. Crispy shrimp on a bed of white cheddar grits, topped with fresh diced tomatoes and green onions. Our catfish and fried chicken are also popular choices.

"It all sounds delicious. Such a difficult decision." Alicia surveyed the menu.

"I'm feeling the same way. Everything looks good," Dallas said. "Can you give us a few more minutes?"

"Certainly. Take your time. I'll come back in a few." Morgan smiled and went to serve more tables.

Alicia turned her attention back to Dallas. "I'll ask again. Do you think he'll come after you?"

Dallas placed her hand in his and planted a kiss on her turned-up palm. "Maybe. I've been getting phone calls from an unknown number. When I answer, whoever it is, says nothing and hangs up."

Alicia reached for her glass of wine and took a sip. "Do you think it's him?"

Dallas shrugged. "I don't know. It's not hard to find out anything about anybody these days. Just Google it." Dallas shook his head. "Maybe I'm being paranoid."

"Maybe you're not. What are you going to do? You can't wait until something happens to get a handle on this situation, Dallas," Alicia said with concern lacing her tone.

"You're right," he said. I think we should head back to Nashville tomorrow, after the last tour I've scheduled. I don't' want this the put a damper on our good time. I might be overreacting from the news that he's out of prison. Shit, even the guy at Karaoke looked like him, just much heavier."

"Well, if you thought that, why didn't we leave? Remember, I asked you that very question because of the way you were reacting to this person."

"I'm not going to hide from my life because I think I'm seeing things." Dallas scanned the crowd. "Besides, we've had security detail since we arrived. Katie insisted."

Alicia took that in for several moments. She nodded. "I not only agree with heading back to Nashville, but I also think we should go back to Houston after your meeting. I know you wanted to stay a few days longer, but we don't know for sure what this Conway person is up to and if your intuition felt that was him at Karaoke, I'd say it's cause for concern. What if he's followed us?"

"Maybe we're both overreacting. Let's not talk about it anymore and focus on each other, and having a great time, okay?"

Alicia gazed into his eyes and gave his hand a squeeze, still feeling a sense of urgency. "Even though I'm upset with you right now, we're in this together."

Alicia's smile covered a multitude of worries. This stalker person wouldn't leave her mind and the fact that Dallas was severely affected disturbed her even more. If she'd known about this situation beforehand, neither one of them would have taken this trip.

Chapter 12

Nashville, Tennessee

Arriving back at the Hermitage, Alicia yawned as she headed straight to the shower. Stepping in, the warm water hit her skin and she moaned in gratitude. Strong hands attacked her curves with exigency. "My god you're beautiful," Dallas whispered.

Her heart pounded against her chest. She could hear his breathing, slow, steady, and wanting. When his hands touched her skin, her body tingled in anticipation of what was to come.

"Relax, baby." Dallas lightly nibbled on her ear lobe which sent a shiver down her spine.

"Dallas, maybe we..."

"Maybe what?" He tightened his grip. I want you, woman. Don't you want me too?"

Alicia leaned her head back into his chest and allowed him to stroke her body with his soapy hands.

"Damn baby, Dallas groaned, his hands traveling around her breasts, arms, around her waist to her firm behind. Alicia melted.

"That's right beautiful, relax. I got you."

"My God," Alicia screamed the moment he slid inside.

Dallas planted a hungry kiss on her lips and smiled. "The feeling is mutual."

* * *

Alicia opened her eyes to morning and Dallas standing in front of the mirror, getting dressed for his meeting. Looking dapper in a crisp, white shirt and a black and red, pinned-striped tie, the black, Armani suit was custom-made for him. His distraction was evident, and worry covered his face.

Alicia threw the covers off her body and slid out of bed. Fumbling with his tie, she covered his hands with hers. "Let me."

Dallas lowered his arms to his sides. "Thanks, baby," he said.

"Honey, we need to address this when we get back. If you feel this man is here, you have an obligation to contact the authorities. If not, I'll have our bags packed so we can leave immediately."

Dallas kissed her gently. "I agree with you, sweetheart. I'll be back in a few hours." He pulled her into a strong, embrace and held on, not wanting to let her go.

Alicia gently nudged him into the hallway. "Things will be fine. Go be great.

When he made it to the elevator, he turned and said, "Don't go anywhere until I get back.

Alicia smiled. "I promise."

She watched him walk down the hall to the elevator. The swag was sexy as hell. Shutting the door, she leaned her head against the frame and let out a long breath, then went to make a cup of tea.

* * *

A light tapping on the door, awoke Alicia from her slumber. She tied the robe tighter about her frame, as she went to the door and peered through the peephole but couldn't make out the image.

"Who is it?" she asked.

"Joel from the front desk, ma'am. I have a package for Mr. Avery."

"You can leave it at the door. I'll get it or Dallas will when he returns."

Conway seethed internally, but regained control. "I've been instructed to hand it to you personally," he said.

Alicia frowned. "Okay, just a second." Hesitantly, she opened the door. Hands pushed Alicia inside, causing her to stumble backward. Before she could get her bearings, a sharp pain traveled through her head, then everything went black.

Chapter 13

"That went well." Katie gathered the documents and tucked them in her briefcase. "I believe we have this in the bag."

Dallas nodded, but he barely heard her. He'd been trying to contact Alicia, but she wasn't answering her phone or his texts. He needed to leave now. Something was wrong.

Katie nudged his shoulder, then asked, "Are you okay? I don't believe you heard a word I said."

Dallas glanced at his phone, then grabbed his briefcase. "Look, Katie, I'm sorry but I need to get back to the hotel. Wrap up everything here and give me a call later." He rushed out of the conference room before she could respond.

"What? Dallas, wait," Katie called, then noticed people gaping in her direction.

Philip Ardmore approached Katie, and asked, "What's going on? We still have documents to sign for Mr. Avery's endorsement deal."

Katie placed her hand over her forehead. After calming herself, she said, "Yes, Mr. Ardmore. We're aware. Dallas had a family emergency. He sends his apologies. Everything's a go. I'll make sure the documents are signed and back to you in the morning. How's that? Please know that Dallas is excited to represent Ardmore Sports."

He shook Katie's hand. "Very well. Tell him that I hope everything is all right."

"I will sir and thank you." Katie took out her phone and texted, Dallas, Call me ASAP. What's going on with you?"

Dallas texted back. "I believe Alicia is in danger."

Katie gasped. "What the hell?" She said her goodbyes and hurried to her car, calling Dallas who answered on the first ring.

"What the hell are you talking about, Dallas?" Katie asked, her anxiety going through the roof.

"Alicia won't respond to my phone calls or texts. I have this feeling deep down, that he's here. I don't want her to be a part of this craziness and I'm going to deal with Conway Ackerman face to face. If he hurts Alicia in any way, I promise that I'll kill him."

"Are you crazy?" Katie asked. "The man is insane, and what about the media?"

"I don't give a rat's ass about the media Katie." He snapped. "I'm shocked that those words even came out of your mouth. Obviously, you're not worried about Alicia or me for that matter. I'll handle this myself."

"Dallas, wait," she yelled.

The dial tone sounded in Katie's ear. She did care about him and Alicia but was scared too. With her eyes on the road, she sped down the highway, while calling 9-1-1.

* * *

Dallas jumped out of the town car before it came to a complete stop. His chest was tight, and he could hardly catch a breath. His long, quick strides, turned into a sprint as he arrived at the elevator.

"Mr. Avery, sir, are you all right?"

"Albert, listen man," Dallas rushed into the elevator. Take me up to my suite now."

"Yes, sir." Albert closed the doors and pressed the Penthouse button. He kept his eyes on Dallas who was clearly panicked. When the elevators opened, Dallas said, "Call the police and tell them to get here fast. It's a matter of life and death. Can you handle that?"

Albert's expression turned frantic. "Yes, sir, Mr. Avery, sir."

Dallas sprinted down the hall. At the door, he went to insert the key card, but noticed the door was ajar. Trepidation rose within him, and he called out, "Alicia, baby, are you in here?"

His heart sped up and panic nearly set in. Dropping his briefcase on the chaise, he slowly walked through the suite. Arriving at the master bedroom, the door was shut, but soft music echoed. Dallas opened the door to find Alicia lying on the bed, still in her black, silk nightgown. She appeared to be sleeping. He dashed to her side, checked her pulse, then wrapped her in his arm, smoothing hair away from her face.

"Alicia, baby," he said touching her face, when a voice said,

"Welcome home," Conway smiled, pointing the shiny, forty-five caliber in his direction.

Dallas quickly turned to see a man dressed in all black, wearing a Mavericks cap.

He gently laid Alicia's head on a pillow, noticing blood on his hand.

"What did you do to her?" Dallas growled.

Conway laughed. "That's a nasty bump on the back of her head, but she'll survive. For now."

Anger boiled within Dallas, but he couldn't act on it. Alicia was hurt, and Conway Ackerman was a crazy son of a bitch. He needed to keep this situation calm, but she needed help right away.

Conway perched in a chair by the window. "You do remember me, don't you?

Dallas glared at him. "I remember you. How could I forget? What do you want, Conway?"

"That's Mr. Ackerman, and what I want is you dead for all the pain you've caused me."

"What? You were the one that committed a crime against me."

"I am your number one fan. Can't you see that?" Conway left his seat and paced the room. "Leave me alone, I got this, Julian," he yelled.

Dallas ignored the statement and kept his attention on Alicia. She still hadn't stirred, and he was past worried. Conway continued to pace, having a conversation with the noise in his head. His voice changed from soft to stone while he waved the gun above his head.

Dallas's cell softly vibrated in his pocket. He closed his eyes and said a prayer.

* * *

Alicia's vision was blurred as she blinked to bring her surrounding into focus. When the haze cleared, Dallas had her in his arms, watching, worry plastering his face. Her head was pounding, but she gave his hand a squeeze. "I'll be all right, baby," she tried to assure him. "The man, I shouldn't have…"

He touched her lips with his finger. "Don't talk. Everything is going to be all right."

"Will it?" Conway snarled. "You don't care about your fans, Dallas Avery. You don't care about me. I lost everything when you had me arrested. All I tried to do was show my adoration, spending tons of money to get the best seats in the house. I should've killed you. There was every opportunity to wipe you off the face of this earth."

Dallas remained quiet, his mind racing trying to figure a way to disarm him. The police were on the way, and he didn't want to do anything to jeopardize Alicia's life or his.

"Can you get Alicia a glass of water, please?"

Conway's eyes darted from him to Alicia. "The Queen has risen," he taunted. "I was hoping she would've gone cold, but it's just as well. You both will be dead soon. I'll bring you both your last meal." His laugh was sinister, as he swept from the room.

Dallas looked down at Alicia and mouthed, "I'm going to get us out of here, baby. I promise."

Alicia's smile was faint, and she said, "I know, baby. We're going to make it out alive."

She drifted off again, which worried him even more. He removed the cell from his jacket pocket when a text from Katie came in. *"The hotel is surrounded with law enforcement. Stay cool."*

He looked at Alicia and whispered, "Help is here."

Alicia let out a breath. "Thank you, God." Dallas closed his eyes and prayed, *"God cover us."*

Chapter 14

Hermitage Hotel -10:00 pm

Red and blue lights flickered in the night. The media stood, cameras ready and journalist broadcasting the event locally, and some, all over the country.

"This is Nora Close from Nashville's WKRN News. I'm standing across the street from The Hermitage Hotel where basketball star, Dallas Avery and his female companion are being held hostage by convicted criminal, Conway Ackerman. We've learned, Ackerman served five years behind bars for the aggravated stalking of the superstar athlete. It's unclear how he tracked down Mr. Avery, however, we are waiting for more details and will give updates as they come in. This is Nora Close, WKRN News. Back to you, George."

Katie pushed through the crowd but was quickly blocked by a brute of a policeman.

He glowered at her. "Stay back, ma'am. You can't enter the hotel."

"But I'm Dallas Avery's agent. I have to get in there," she said loud enough to draw the attention of some reporters standing behind her, causing them to move in closer. "I'm the one who called in for help."

The officer gave her and the media an angry glare. He said through clenched teeth, "No one, not even Dallas Avery's agent can cross the line. Stand back."

Katie rolled her eyes and stepped back into a swarm of questions and media frenzy.

* * *

Anna watched in horror, the story unfolding on the screen. She picked up the phone and called Katie, who was not only Dallas's agent, but a family friend. Katie answered on the first ring. "Miss Anna, I was…"

Before Katie could complete the sentence, Anna said, "Conway Ackerman is out of prison?"

"Yes, ma'am. I …."

"How in the world did he find my son, all the way in Nashville?"

Katie paused, then said, "Miss Anna, social media and the internet, period. It's not hard to find out anything about anybody. Especially, someone with celebrity status like Dallas.

Anna paced the floor of the family room. "That is true. Are there any updates other than what's on television?"

"As far as I know, there isn't any change. The police wouldn't tell me anything, and they won't let me through to get to the hotel."

A few seconds of silence passed, then Anna said, "I want to be on the next plane to Nashville. There's no way I can sit here knowing my son is in danger."

"Miss Anna, maybe you shouldn't…"

"I'll be in Nashville, camping out on the lawn until my son comes out of that hotel in one piece."

There was no way Dallas' mother was going to change her mind. "Yes, ma'am, I'll make the arrangements and email you the details."

"That would be great, Katie. Thank you."

"You're welcome, Miss Anna. See you soon."

After disconnecting the call, Anna kneeled. As tears formed in her eyes, she prayed,

"Lord, I need you right this moment. Watch over my son. Bring him out of this situation alive. Cover and protect him Lord. Amen."

* * *

Hermitage Hotel – 2:00 am

Hours passed and Conway's personality would alternate from himself to alter ego Julian. He'd started drinking alcohol from the bar, going off on tantrums, and even putting the gun to his own head, threatening to blow his brains out but he never pulled the trigger, to Dallas' dismay.

Finally, Conway returned with a tray of two bottles of water, crackers, and an apple.

He shoved the tray into Dallas' chest. "Bona Appetit. Make it last because there will be no more."

Gazing out of the window, Conway saw the police cars and lights flashing.

"The Calvary has arrived to rescue you, Mr. Avery. Too bad this will be the recovery of two dead bodies," he said pointing the gun in their direction.

Dallas moved between Conway and his path to Alicia. "It's me you want. Release her, Conway. She needs medical attention. I'll call off the authorities if you let my woman go."

Conway lowered the gun to his side. The crazed expression was replaced with a smirk. "Your begging is entertaining."

For reasons that couldn't be explained, Conway threw the gun on the chair behind him. Dallas watched, calculating the best time to make his move. He looked down to find Alicia watching him. She nodded.

Dallas cleared his throat. "I need to help Alicia to the bathroom," he said sternly.

Conway moved towards them. "She can relieve herself right where she is and lay in the stench," he snarled.

"Come on, Conway, you're not that stone-hearted, are you? Allow her to use the bathroom, at least."

Conway tilted his head to one side and stepped forward. His smile was replaced with an angry glare, and he said, "So, you think you're the one calling the shots now? You people don't know how to stay in your place."

Dallas's body grew warm with anger. "You people? What the hell do you mean by that?"

"You know what I mean," Conway said with a cackle.

Dallas pretended to lift Alicia off the bed. Instead, he faked a left swing using her body, so that her feet connected with Conway's jaw. Alicia rolled over to the other side of the bed, sat up and grabbed the gun, pointing it in their direction

The bodies rolled from side to side, until Conway abandoned any attempt to get free. Instead, he wrapped his hands around Dallas throat. Adrenaline kicked in and Dallas pried Conway's hands from his neck, as they continued to struggle.

Alicia screamed. "Get off him."

Conway ignored the demand and Alicia fired twice, each bullet striking him in the back of the head. His body stilled. Dallas pushed him to the side. He sat up breathing heavily, gazing at Alicia, giving her a thumbs up. "Nice shot. Thanks, babe."

Suddenly, the police burst through the open door. Alicia was froze, her hand gripping the metal piece. A police-officer slowly approached her. "It's okay, ma'am. You're safe. Hand me the gun."

Alicia remained trance-like. Everything seemed to move in slow motion. Her mind wandered from past to present. A voice brought her back to the here and now.

With shaking hands, she dropped the gun on the floor and fell into Dallas' arms. He held her tight. "I'm here. It's over, baby." He brushed the tears from her eyes. "Let's get you to the hospital. I love you."

She touched his face and said, "I love you, too."

* * *

Cameras flashed as soon as Dallas and Alicia appeared, but no one could get a clear image because she was fully covered by a sheet. Dallas insisted. The paramedics put her into an ambulance. Dallas was on their heels while reporters swarmed them from every angle.

"Dallas, will you give a statement?" a reporter asked.

"Dallas, who is the woman?" another asked.

"Dallas, did you kill Conway Ackerman?"

He ignored every question and stepped up into the vehicle, taking Alicia's hand in his.

Putting the back of her hand to his cheek, he kissed it and said, "You're going to be fine, baby."

When the ambulance doors shut, Alicia gazed into his eyes. "I know. Thank God for bringing us through."

Dallas smoothed the hair away from her face. "Yes, I'm thankful."

Alicia closed her eyes. "The media is going to have a heyday with all of this. I heard all the questions being thrown out there."

"I'll deal with that part when the time comes. You're my main concerned right now. Just relax, baby. We'll be at the hospital in a few minutes."

Alicia nodded. Her mind wandered to what could've happened if she hadn't put those bullets in Conway Ackerman.

Chapter 15

Nashville, Tennessee – Vanderbilt University Medical Center

Arriving at Vanderbilt University Medical Center, the medical staff quickly gathered Alicia, and pushed the stretcher to the examination room. Dallas followed close behind but was stopped once he was about to step inside.

"I'm sorry, Mr. Avery. Only authorized, medical personnel are allowed inside. My name is Dr. Collins, and I'll be back to give you an update. She's in good hands." He gave Dallas shoulder a squeeze. "Try to relax."

Dallas watched until Alicia was no longer visible. He looked at the doctor and rubbed his head with his hands. "I'm going to go get some air. I'll be back."

Dr. Collins nodded and went back into the examination room.

Dallas was met by a swarm of reporters when he stepped outside the hospital. He let out a long breath as he was bombarded with questions coming from all directions.

"Dallas, how did Conway Ackerman find you?" "Who pulled the trigger?" Is the lady your love interest?" "Who is she?"

Two women pushed their way through the crowd. Dallas sighed with relief when his mother and Katie rushed towards him. He embraced Anna, ignoring the barrage of questions. "Mom, what are you doing here?"

Cameras flashed as he helped both women inside. Anna eyes traveled the length of her son's body before she asked, "Do you think after what I saw on the news, that I wouldn't be here to check on my son?"

Katie, whose ivory skin had flushed a red, nodded. "Nothing I said could stop her mission to get here."

Security led them to the VIP wing of the hospital, out of the public eye. Dallas led Anna to a cushioned chair and sat next to her.

"Thank you," Dallas said, wrapping his arms around her petite frame. His father wasn't much taller, and people always wondered where Dallas' height came from.

"Are you hurt?" she asked, placing a hand on his chest.

"I'm fine, Mom."

"How's your friend?" Anna continued to quiz.

Dallas sighed. "She's being checked out by the doctor now. I'm waiting to get an update."

"Why didn't you tell me Conway Ackerman was out of prison, son?'

"I didn't want you to worry." He stood and went to the window, to see a slew of nosey reporters still gathered outside.

"Are they ever going to leave?" Dallas shook his head.

"I'll handle it," Katie said, heading to the door.

Dallas rushed over and pulled Katie into a hug. "Thanks. Listen, I'm sorry for the way I spoke to you earlier. I was out of my mind and wasn't thinking clearly."

Katie stepped back and held his hand in hers. "I didn't take it personally."

"You're the best," Dallas said, kissing her on the cheek.

Dr. Collins entered the waiting room, and Dallas quickly approached him. "How is she, Doc? Is she okay?" Anna stepped towards the two men.

"She'll be all right. The concussion is serious, so we're going to keep her for a couple of days. You can go see her now. She's been asking for you. Room three-forty-five.

"Thanks, Doc. Oh, this is my mother," Dallas said, shaking the doctor's hand.

"Pleased to meet you, ma'am," he said, extending his hand to her.

Anna nodded. "Good to meet you doctor and thank you."

Hand in hand, Dallas and his mother walked down the sanitized hallway.

"So, are you going to introduce me to the woman in your life?"

Dallas stopped and turned his mother to face him. "No disrespect, Mom, but I don't think this is a good time right now. With all that she's been through… this isn't the right time or place. I'll have Katie take you back to the hotel."

Katie stepped forward, while adjusting the Ralph Lauren Bellport tote on her shoulder. "That sounds good because your mother is tired and could use some rest. Right, Miss Anna?"

"Very well, son," Anna said flatly. "This is going nowhere. I will tell you that I'm not happy with you right now, but I'll leave it be. I'll have Katie book me a flight home tomorrow."

"Mom, please understand. I promise to put it all out on the table when the time is right." He hugged her tightly. "I'm glad you're here, Mom."

"I'm glad to be here, too son, and thank God you and this mystery woman are safe."

***

Alicia sipped a cup of tea with honey and lemon. She was more than ready to be released after a three-day hospital stay. The vision of Conway Ackerman lying dead on the hotel floor, wouldn't leave her mind, no matter how hard she tried to forget.

Taking a life was something she never wanted to do, but it was necessary to save the life of the man she loved. She would do it all again if she had to. The whole series of events still felt like a dream. In deep thought, she didn't realize Dallas had entered the room.

"Hey, baby," he said, pulling a chair close to her bed. He leaned down to kiss her before sitting down. "How are you feeling?"

Alicia gazed into his eyes. "Still have a slight headache and my body hurts like I've been run over by a truck, but I'm thankful to be alive."

Dallas gently squeezed her hand. "Me too, baby. Did you eat your breakfast?"

"I had a boiled egg, toast, and tea. Not very appetizing."

He touched her face. "I'll make sure you have whatever you crave when I get you out of here. I want you to know that my mother is here. She wanted to meet you, but I chose against it for now."

Alicia nodded. "Did you tell her about us?"

Dallas frowned, shifting in his chair. "What do you mean?"

She tilted her head, giving him a side-eyed glance. "You know what I mean. What does she know about me?"

"I told her you were beautiful, smart and independent."

"Did you tell her I was much older than you?"

"No."

"Did you let her know that I'm not a gold digger and that I live a very comfortable life?"

"Baby." Dallas sighed. "I said, nothing."

Alicia sighed. "I'm sorry. I don't mean to grill you, sweetheart. Honestly, I'm still reeling from everything that's happened. Don't get me wrong, I don't regret what I did, but…" She leaned her head back on the pillow. "When can I get out of here?"

"The doctor will be in shortly. Hopefully you'll be released in a couple of days. He wants to review some test results first."

"Will we be able to leave Nashville the minute he says it's a go?"

"The police have a few more questions for us before closing the investigation, then we're free to go. I'm taking you back to Houston to recuperate. Are you okay with that?"

"Do I have a choice as far as the police are concerned? I don't want to talk about this ordeal anymore." Alicia looked away and sighed.

"No, we don't. Baby, everything's all right. I got you, okay?"

"I know you do," she sighed. "I'm so over this, Dallas. I want things to be normal again, but something tells me we are forever changed."

"You're right, baby. This has altered us both in more ways than one. My love for you has grown in leaps and bounds. I'd trade places with you in a heartbeat. Together, we'll get through this. I promise to be right by your side now and always."

Alicia couldn't contain her tears. Dallas sat on the bed beside her and pulled her into his strong embrace. She knew, at that moment, she loved this man with all her heart and wanted to be with him for life.

* * *

Perched against a mound of pillows, Alicia wrote in her journal. Thoughts from her time with Dallas, to the events that occurred over the past days, were a constant in her mind. The trauma from the hostage situation they'd experience at the hands of Conway Ackerman, shed a bright light on the fact that their lives hung in the balance, and only by the grace of God, did they make it out alive. For the first time, he'd kept her in the dark to a part of his past that was prevalent to their well-being. If she'd known, would the outcome have been different?

As the black ink covered the pages, realization of the shortness of life pulled at her heartstrings. She knew that Dallas Avery was her one and only. There could be no other that made her feel the way he did. The thought of living life without him was something she wasn't willing to do. Or was she?

Closing the black, book with the words, *My Release,* in gold calligraphy, she placed the pen in the side pocket, clicking the lock in place. Opening the side drawer, Alicia removed the small tote, holding a few magazines and put the journal between them. She settled back into the pillows and closed her eyes.

Chapter 16

Nashville, Tennessee

Dallas stepped out of Philip Ardmore's office into a sea of reporters. His feelings were conflicted and the memories bittersweet. If he didn't have to come back to Nashville, he would've never stepped foot in this city again, if he could've predicted what events would unfold. Scanning the faces, he turned to Katie and nodded. "Let's do this."

"Are you sure?" Katie looked up at him. "I told you I can take this if you want."

Dallas shook his head. "They've already heard from you. It's me they want to hear from. This will be the one and only time, though."

"Good afternoon, everyone," Katie said. "This is quite unexpected, seeing you all outside of Ardmore Enterprises. At any rate, we know why you're here and Dallas has agreed to answer a few questions." She motioned to Dallas who was standing next to her in a charcoal gray, Virgil Abloh suit, a Black designer from Illinois. He exhaled a long breath and held up his hand to quiet the crowd.

"The media can be brutal and uncaring," he said. "I'm aware of my celebrity status and have been in the public eye long enough to know how it works. You want to know and will get the story by any means necessary. I'll take a few questions. I may or may not answer them, but to be clear, this is the last time I will speak on this subject."

The cameras flashed, hands raised, and the chatter began.

"Dallas, John Cooley, Action News, Memphis," one said. "How did Conway Ackerman know you were in Nashville?"

Dallas cleared his throat. "I'm surprised you're asking that question. We all know it's not hard to find anything about anybody when you surf the web. The media," he said glaring at the reporter, "sneak around, snapping photos of celebrities' whereabouts all the time. Besides, it wasn't a secret that I'd be here in Nashville."

"Karen O'Shea from CNN. Who is the woman that was with you, and did she fire the shots that ended Conway Ackerman's life?"

Silence filled the air. The million-dollar question had been asked. Dallas knew it was more about who the woman on his arm was than both of them almost losing their lives.

"What everyone is dying to know," Dallas said. "She is the love of my life. I wouldn't be standing here today if she didn't pull the trigger. Let's not forget, she was hurt too. Spent two days in the hospital with a concussion. I owe her everything."

"Why won't you tell us her name?" a reporter asked. Dallas ignored the question.

"How is she recovering from the concussion?" another reporter asked.

He relaxed for a moment. "She's coming along well. Thanks for asking. Wow, that was the best question I've had so far."

The crowd chuckled and Dallas smiled. "I'll take one more question, then I have to get to the airport.

"Marvin Porter, TMZ. Rumor has it that the woman in your life is almost twice your age. Can you elaborate?" The man grinned as others around him glanced in his direction, then Dallas'.

Dallas' face flushed with anger. "No comment."

The same reporter stepped forward again and pressed. "Come on,

Dallas. Tell us about the woman you say is the love of your life. Don't you want the world to know?"

Dallas glared at the reporter. "Tread lightly," he warned.

Ears and eyes were open wanting to know more about Dallas' love interest. TMZ was known for digging into the personal lives of others to make a spectacle.

The reporter stepped back. He'd done what he came to do and that was bring light to the fact that Dallas Avery was in a relationship with a woman old enough to be his mother.

"No more questions," Dallas said, and moved through the crowd to the awaiting town car.

***

"I wanted to face the media and put this to bed," Dallas said fuming. "It's obvious they were more interested in my love life than Conway Ackerman." He ran his hand down the side of his face and closed his eyes.

"I'm sorry," Katie said, "I should've handled it."

Dallas shook his head. "It's not your fault. I'm the one who wanted to address the media, well, we both know how TMZ is. All I know is they better leave Alicia alone or all hell will break loose."

Katie nodded. "You'll have to tell Alicia what happened."

"No doubt," Dallas said. "I'll never keep her in the dark about anything again.

Dallas rested his head back on the headrest. He closed his eyes knowing he'd be home and in Alicia's arms soon.

Waiting for his flight in the VIP lounge, he removed his cell from his jacket pocket and called the one person that made his world complete.

* * *

Since they'd returned to Houston, Dallas had waited on Alicia hand and foot. He had to slide back to Nashville to wrap up business with Philip Ardmore. It was nice to have some alone time because she needed to clear her head and figure out what she wanted to do pertaining to their relationship and her life, period. However, the hostage drama and everything else they'd gone through together, only brought them closer in every aspect of the word.

Alicia sat at the kitchen island, thumbing through the newspaper, when her cell rang. She smiled when she saw Dallas' name cross the screen.

"Hey baby. I miss you," he said.

"Hey you. I miss you too," she cooed. "When will you be home?"

"Soon," he said. "I'm at the airport now. It's only been three days, but it feels like three weeks. I can't wait to get back to you. Are you all right?"

"I've been a good girl," she teased. "Following the doctor's orders and yours. How was the meeting?"

"Everything went well. I won't have to come back to Nashville any time soon."

"I'm happy to hear that. I'd like to close the book and never return again."

"You won't have to worry about that. I have a gift for you." He changed the subject.

"You do? What is it?" Alicia asked in an excited tone.

"Just a little something, something. I think you'll like it."

"A hint?" Alicia quizzed.

"You'll see when I get home. Okay, baby, I'll be boarding soon," Dallas said.

Alicia sighed. "Your lips are sealed, eh?"

"For now," Dallas chuckled. "Until I taste yours."

"Smooth." Alicia giggled. "Safe travels. I can't wait until you get home. I love you."

"Love you, too." Dallas disconnected the call, feeling a sense of relief. Making Alicia happy was all that mattered to him.

Houston, Texas

Dallas entered his condo close to midnight. The slightly, dimmed light led the way to the living room. He placed the gift wrapped, floral box on the ottoman in front of him, and flopped down on the sofa, closing his eyes. Exhaustion bared down on his body, and he needed to unwind a bit before going into the bedroom. Waking Alicia was the last thing he wanted to do.

The curvaceous image appeared in his peripheral vision and slid into the space beside him. She caressed his thigh gently. "I missed you."

Dallas rested his head on her shoulder and inhaled the sweet scent of perfume. His eyes followed the slinky, red nightie that brushed the middle of her thigh. He embraced her. "I missed you too. How are you feeling?"

"I'm much better now that you're here. How was your trip? Traveling back to Nashville wasn't easy I'm sure." She glanced at the colorful, wrapped box in front of her.

"From a business perspective, all went well. We tied up all the particulars and I'm satisfied and excited with what's to come." He leaned forward and grabbed hold of the box.

"For you." He smiled. I saw this in Nordstrom's window, and it called to me."

Alicia put the box on her lap. She carefully removed the white bow and silky wrapping paper. Opening the box and pulling back the tissue paper, she gasped. "

"Dallas," she said lifting the orange, Gucci trench coat with round, gold buttons and a matching Double G buckle belt. The large, gold-handle umbrella had an orange backdrop, showcasing yellow and lavender calla lilies.

"Oh my god, Dallas. This is the coat." She stood and put it on.

"I know," Dallas said. "I saw how you stared at it and wondered why you didn't get it."

Alicia buttoned and belted the coat. She opened the umbrella and twirled around. "How do I look?" she asked.

"As beautiful as I knew you would." Dallas stood and pulled her close. "I love you," he said.

"Thank you, sweetheart. I love you too. Now," Alicia said, "Did anything else happen? I feel you're leaving something out. Correct me if I'm wrong." She removed the coat and placed it on top of the box. She held his hands, and they both sat down.

Dallas frowned. "What?" he teased.

"I'm a big girl, baby. I'm sensing something happened that you're not telling me."

Dallas nodded. "You're right. I had a run in with the media. When we came out of Philip Ardmore's office, reporters were everywhere. They started right in on Conway Ackerman and us."

Alicia sat up and asked, "Us? Why?"

"TMZ did their usual digging for the sake of gossip."

Alicia frowned. "What did they dig up?"

Dallas sighed. "Well, our age difference was the main attraction. They didn't even ask about our hostage situation. I wouldn't entertain the questions. It's none of their business."

Alicia nodded. "I don't want either of our lives to become difficult because of our relationship. We both have enough on our plates. Maybe I should go back to Chicago."

A shocked expression covered Dallas' face. Cupping her face in his hands, he bore into her eyes. "No. I'd go crazy if you left because of what the media has to say. Don't you understand that I want to be with you, woman? You're everything I want and need." He moved in and planted kisses on her cheek and neck. She stirred, her body reacting to his touch.

Alicia rested her head on his chest. She wanted to pour her feelings into his heart, along with the insecurity and self-doubt. There were so many times when she felt inadequate, let alone the age difference. But she didn't want to be anywhere else. Being with Dallas unleashed a sensual side that raised her to new heights. Why couldn't she accept it? But he was young, handsome, talented, and wealthy. A professional athlete for God's sake. What could he possibly see in her?

"A penny for your thoughts." Dallas lifted her chin, gazing into her green eyes.

Alicia exhaled a long breath. If she was honest with herself, she'd throw caution to the wind and let things be. "I'm sorry, Dallas." She blinked to keep the tears from falling. "I love you so much, but I keep asking myself, *are you sure it's me you want?* I mean, you could have any woman, younger and more beautiful than me. I'm just saying." She attempted to look away, but he held her face firmly.

"I can only continue to show you what you mean to me. Empty your mind and let me take care of you in every way."

Alicia dipped her head, then sighed "All right, but you know I do have to go back to Chicago eventually. My life is there…" she paused.

Dallas knelt in front of her and pulled her to him. "Your life is with me. Please stay."

"Oh, Dallas," Alicia's eyes watered, his words pulling at her heartstring."

"Please, baby."

"All right, I'll stay. I do have to handle some business back home since I'm going to be here in Houston a while longer. But it's only a phone call away."

Dallas jumped up and did a fist pump, yelling, "Yes!" He started to pick her up, then stopped, remembering she was still in recovery mode.

He bent down and kissed her with so much passion, it took her breath away. He gazed into her eyes. "You've made me the happiest man in the world."

ABOUT THE AUTHOR

Christine Pauls is a Women's Fiction author and is a native of Wilmington, Delaware.

She penned her first novel, To Begin Again, in 2012. Her books include, Belinda's Song, One Good Thing, and her Love Series, Love for Granted, Never Too Late and The Love You Save, her newest release.

She is a beta-reader/editor as well as diving into the field of developmental editing in the future.

The mother of two and grandmother of three is an accountant by day in the banking industry.

You can find her books on Amazon and Barnes and Noble websites, her hometown's public library and independent bookstores in her area.

Her website is: www.christinepauls.com

LOVE FOR GRANTED

Daybreak peeked through the sheer shades covering the window in the master bedroom of the Harlem apartment on 136th Street. Adina rubbed her eyes, opening them to focus on the clock perched on the corner of her nightstand; five forty-five a.m.

Her man's arm was draped across her waist as he snored softly. His close-cut beard brushed the nape of her neck. Gently, she moved out of his embrace. He didn't stir.

She entered the bathroom, stopping to stare at her reflection in the mirror before turning on the warm water, splashing it on her face with open palms.

From the moment they met, sparks flew between her and Deion, the man in the bedroom. Although she vowed never to involve herself in a long-term romance again, after a two-year relationship with Qudair who proved monogamy wasn't in his vocabulary, the chemistry between them overrode her common sense.

She stood in the bathroom's entryway, leaned against the frame, and watched the object of her affection. Her body grew warm as she absorbed Deion's dark, mocha skin and perfectly chiseled body. His bald head shined, and his beard with a few specs of premature gray sparkled. Adina was in love with this man and he with her. Yet, a tinge of sadness covered her soul.

One year of bliss and she'd have to break the news that her singing career was taking a favorable turn. Her manager, Maxwell Alston, called about a six-month gig in Europe which could lead to a recording contract. It was a dream realized. To sing for a living was all she'd ever wanted to do. She couldn't pass up the opportunity, but how would she tell him? She shook off her anxiety and moved back into the bedroom, and sat on the side of the bed, next to Deion, who still hadn't stirred.

Deion, thirty-two, was a NYPD police officer at the 13th Precinct. He'd been on the force for eight years. They met at Cocoa's in Harlem, a dinner club where she performed on the weekends. The attraction was instant when their eyes met while Adina did her rendition of Erykah Badu's, *Love of My Life*.

During a brief intermission, he approached her at the bar, introduced himself, and bought her a drink. Their conversation led to more time spent with each other, and a year later, they were living together in a full-blown relationship.

Now, her time had come at the age of thirty. Singing was her passion. Being a loan officer at Chase Manhattan paid the bills. She didn't know how to talk to Deion about the tour offer because she'd be going into the discussion with her mind made up. This was her chance to fulfill a life-long dream. It was only for six months, and she was sure they could make it through.

Adina touched his shoulder and called, "Deion, love, it's six o' clock. Time to get up, sweetheart."

Deion stretched, opening his eyes. "Hey, baby, I'm up. Come here."

"No, no, no, Officer." She laughed. "Don't start none, won't be none. We both have a busy day. I have a show tonight; remember? I must make sure I leave work on time and go straight to rehearsal. Showtime's at eight o'clock."

"I know baby, and I'll be there. My shift's over at four, and I'm off tomorrow. It's the first time in two months. The joy of being a cop." Deion yawned, stretching his arms above his head. "Let me do my push-ups while you hit the shower. I won't sneak in and join you." He snickered.

Adina tightened her robe, giving Deion a sly grin. She kissed him on the cheek, and he brushed his lips against hers, holding her in a tight embrace, while gently squeezing her buttocks.

"Okay," she said pushing away, "Let me take my shower so you can get in next. I'll make coffee while you get ready. We'll have to pick up something for breakfast on the go. I love you, baby."

"Love you, too." Deion dropped to the floor and began his set.

SYNOPSIS

Deion and Adina are young and in love. Their bond is unbreakable. That is until an opportunity arises for Adina that will boost her passion to sing into another atmosphere, kissing her nine to five as a loan officer, goodbye.

Deion, a police officer for the NYPD doesn't feel the same and what happens next will test the strength of their relationship to its breaking point. Will they fight through it together or live life apart? Who is taking love for granted?

Never Too Late

Raelene nursed the vodka and cranberry with a slice of lime as she scanned the Italian-inspired décor of the restaurant and watched the patrons enjoying animated conversations and easy laughter. As she opened her compact to freshen her plum lipstick, her gaze connected with her six-feet, brown-eyed son the moment he entered the restaurant. The medals that adorned his shoulder were expanding.

Maybe that's the news. A smile lifted the corners of her lips but quickly stilled when she realized he wasn't alone.

The tall, striking, middle-aged man in uniform, with a complexion that mirrored her son's deep brown skin tone, had an array of medals along his shoulder that were near blinding. His panther-like gait was more confident than arrogant and drew the attention of many of the women in the establishment as he followed Andre to the reserved table. Raelene's breath caught in her throat. Her body tingled in places she thought were dead and gone. Try as she might, she could not look away;

her eyes remained fixed on the handsome stranger.

"Hey, Mom." Andre kissed her left cheek, allowing her gaze to remain focused on the drop-dead gorgeous stranger right behind him.

"This is Lieutenant Gregory Banks. Lieutenant, meet my mother, Raelene Thompson."

"It's a pleasure to meet you, Ms. Thompson." Gregory's baritone voice was remnant of the maestro Barry White. He removed his hat, revealing close-cut hair that glistened with hints of gray. His skin was smooth with chocolatey goodness and his eyes, light brown and piercing. The lieutenant accepted the hand Raelene extended and pressed a velvety kiss on the backside, causing her Pandora's Box to pound. His eyes swept over her as she tried to form words to speak.

"Mom?" Andre touched her shoulder.

"Oh, um, yes, nice to meet you, Lieutenant and please, call me Raelene."

"Call me Greg, please." He smiled, and in that one motion, Raelene realized exactly what this was all about.

She glanced at her son, giving him "that look" since his sly grin was firmly in place.

Andre and Greg moved in unison; Andre slid into the seat next to her, while Greg took the one across.

Andre whipped out his cell and frowned. "Excuse me. I have to take this call. I'll be right back. Mom, could you order me the Shrimp Fra Diavolo," he asked, tapping the menu to highlight the entrée. He kissed her again on the cheek. "Thanks."

Raelene gave him a questioning glare. His phone hadn't rung or even vibrated. Andre made a hasty exit before she could object, his grin widening with each step toward his scheme being complete. She took a longer sip, more like a gulp, of the pinkish liquid as Greg's intense gaze stayed focused on her. She could strangle Andre for what was an obvious matchmaking ploy.

Well, played, son. Well, played.

SYNOPSIS

Raelene Thompson was hardly entertaining the thought of having a man in her life. That is, until her son, Andre, slyly introduces her to the handsome Lieutenant Gregory Banks, his commanding officer. The attraction is instant. However, after suffering a heartbreak that shadows her to this day, she feels the need to guard her heart and preserve her way of life.

Gregory is determined to share his life with someone who will help him make up for all the years he lost being committed to something that can never fill a void. As much as they seem to be the perfect pair, their life's goals couldn't be more diametrically opposed. It's never too late to find love, but are they willing to take the risk?

The Love You Save

The striking man demanded Miranda's attention, even as her gaze slid to the female at his side. The effect was like a gut punch. Miranda clung to the handlebars of the shopping cart where she stood in the produce section of Kroger's. She couldn't get her feet to move, even if it meant saving her life.

The blonde haired, blue-eyed, Caucasian woman with a small waist and large, obviously altered breasts, clutched the hand of a man whose chiseled features and dark-chestnut skin was the mirror image of her husband. In his arms, was an adorable girl with caramel complexion, hazel eyes, and curly, sandy brown hair. She appeared to be at least three years old and was a picture-perfect resemblance to her father.

Miranda pushed her cart closer to the trio, then pulled a plastic bag from its roll and filled it with apples. Lifting her gaze, and focusing up on them, certainty hit her like a bolt of lightning. It was Curtis.

The man glanced in her direction, and their eyes met. His eyes widened, then darted to the female at his side.

"Miranda." His tone was tense. "What are you doing here?"

His betrayal and this ridiculous situation paralyzed her entire being.

"Curtis?" Tears burned her eyes, but she refused to allow them to fall. "What is this?" She pointed at the woman and child.

"Baby, I, I can explain," he stuttered as an older couple passed them pushing an empty cart. The woman cautiously removed the little girl from his arms and stood behind him.

"You can explain?" Miranda held up her hand in a stopping motion. "There's no need. I'm not blind, you double-life living cheating bastard, and you." She waved to the woman behind him, whose eyes were laced with fear. "Who the hell are you and why are you with my husband?" Her voice rose an octave, causing people to stare in their direction.

The woman blinked. She opened her mouth to speak but Curtis interrupted.

"We'll talk about this later, Miranda. Go to the car, Tracy."

The woman quickly stepped, with the little girl in tow, to the exit and out the door.

"Are you kidding me?" Miranda glared at Curtis. "Talk about what later? The fact that you're a no-good son of a bitch?" Miranda spun around, leaving her cart full of items and ran out of the store.

***

Moments later, she sat inside her car, gripping the steering wheel, trying to catch her breath. As tears poured down her cheeks, she pulled her shoulder length, black hair into a tight bun. "Twelve years of dedication and this…." she screamed. Curtis was supposed to be away at a conference in Houston, but his lies came full circle on this day. She regained what little composure she could and drove off in a flood of blinding tears. Somehow, she made it to their two-story, Craftsman home without having an accident.

The Jeep Cherokee screeched to a halt. Miranda jumped out and dashed to the front door. Her hands shook violently as multiple attempts to insert the key finally connected. Once inside, she ran upstairs to the master suite, and threw herself across the bed, releasing agonizing sobs which soon turned into rage. She rushed to the closet, yanked his expensive clothes off the hangers and threw them on the floor. Miranda felt like reenacting the scene from the movie, *Waiting to Exhale* where Angela Basset dumped her husband's clothing in the trash can and struck a match. But that would solve nothing.

Curtis and Miranda were college sweethearts who fell madly in love and made a vow for life. They worked as a team to afford the comfortable life they lived. Both had successful careers in law and advertising. The twins, Candace, and Cameron were in private school. The beautiful home was in one of the most prestigious developments in Atlanta. *How could Curtis do this to her, to their children, to their family?*

SYNOPSIS

Twelve years of marriage to her college sweetheart ends the day Miranda Norwood comes face to face with her husband's other family. Time passes, but the scars from that life-changing day have hardened her heart and love becomes a distant memory. When her friend sets her up on a blind date with a handsome, HR manager, Roy Grander, sparks fly, and Miranda's wall comes down just enough for her to peer over the top.

The handsome man is a fascinating puzzle she longs to solve. Grappling with devastating guilt from the past has kept Roy stuck, but Miranda strikes a chord of longing in his heart. As much as he tries to fight it, his will to resist the insatiable desire for her is slipping through his hands. Can two people, dealing with issues that keep them from moving forward, find a love that will save them?

One Good Thing

The torrential downpour hit the roof with force. Madelyn almost fell on her backside as she slid, teetering back and forth to place a bucket for the water that was trickling from the cracked ceiling above. The house had been her grandmother's for thirty plus years and now, six months after her death; she was there, trying to figure out what the heck she was going to do with it.

"I can't believe I have two sisters. Acting so high and mighty they won't help me fix up the place," Madelyn mumbled. "They the ones with the money."

Georgina and Nola left the small town of Lula, Mississippi, five years ago, moving up north to Harlem, New York, to pursue singing careers. Madelyn, the youngest sister, was left the responsibility of caring for their mother Ophelia and Grandmother Estelle.

I'm sick of this, Madelyn thought while mopping the large puddle. It was hard to believe she was just thirty for how beat up she felt from working her fingers to the bones trying to keep things afloat. Her beauty was hidden behind the dingy white uniform, old nurse shoes and untamed thick black hair that she kept braided under a scarf. Her body was a shapely size twelve on her five-foot-six frame, and her dark skin shone with Vaseline. People said she looked like the actress Cicely Tyson.

Madelyn worked as a seamstress for Miss Bessie's Boutique in town, a job she'd had since the age of sixteen, and she was one of the best at it. She also cleaned houses on some weekends and did ironing for a couple of white families her mother used to work for on the outskirts of town. It was back-breaking work, but Madelyn had to support herself and take care of her mother. She didn't even have a high school education; she dropped out in the tenth grade to work for Miss Bessie full time. If she could get the house fixed up a bit, maybe it could be sold, or even rented out so she could make some kind of profit. Nana didn't owe anything on it, so that money would be hers straight out. But Mama said no matter which way it went, the profits would have to be split between everybody, and unfortunately that included her nowhere to be found sisters.

The forest green Chevy came to an abrupt stop, smoke coughing from the exhaust. Madelyn jumped out and rushed to the mailbox. Her sisters promised to send a money order for one-hundred and fifty dollars to help with patching up that leaky roof. She'd taken that money from her own account and really needed it back in there to pay her own bills. She opened the rusty flap, pulled out the small stack and anxiously thumbed through it.

"Where is it?" Madelyn panicked. There was nothing from her sisters, and she was fuming. "This is gonna be the death of me."

She stormed inside the three-bedroom red brick ranch house and threw the mail on the kitchen table in a huff.

"Georgina or Nola won't even return my calls. And where is that money they was supposed to send over two weeks ago, Mama?" Madelyn's voice rose a higher than normal octave as she paced back and forth.

"Oh girl, hush and sit down somewhere! You know they not gonna do a darn thing!" Ophelia shouted, startling her daughter. "When they left Lula, they left everything behind that reminded them of this place and that included me and you. You just dumb enough to keep thinking they gonna drop their high and mighty lives for us. They don't call me on a regular. What make you think they gonna keep their word to you?"

***

Ophelia was a five-foot-tall, light-skinned, plump woman with snow white shoulder-length hair that still showed remnants of the burnt orange that it used to be. Her hazel-colored eyes were a gift from her Creole mother, who fell in love and married Nathan Brown, a black man from Mississippi. They'd send their daughter to spend summers in his hometown of Lula with her cousin Julie, Nathan's sister's daughter throughout her childhood.

Ophelia Brown was eighteen when she first lay eyes on Charlie

Johnson. He was singing in the church choir; his baritone voice sounded like the soothing rhythm of a saxophone. They fell in love, married after one year, and together had three daughters, Georgina, Nola and then Madelyn, who she gave birth to years later, calling her a "change of life" baby because she certainly thought that she was done having children as she was approaching fifty. Charlie was a janitor at Nelson Boyd Elementary School and provided for his wife and three girls on that salary. They never wanted for anything.

The couple was married forty-five years when Charlie passed away suddenly of a massive heart attack. He was outside working on his old pickup truck when he collapsed to the ground. It was a devastating blow to the family, but it didn't stop Georgina and Nola from leaving not long after. With them gone, Madelyn had to give up the small three-room apartment she rented over Miss Bessie's and move back home to care for her mother and grandmother. She never felt the same about her sisters after that.

"So what I'm supposed to do, Mama? I can't do this all by myself. We can't afford to take care of this house and Nana's even with both our incomes. I could only get that roof patched up and it's only temporary. I need to get the house rented or sold before we go broke. Georgina and Nola don't care about nobody but themselves." Tears threatened to fall from Madelyn's eyes from the thought.

Ophelia watched her daughter feeling a sense of guilt. She desired much more for her baby girl, but Madelyn was always the responsible one, the one she could depend on. Her daughter was right; those other two did leave without a thought or care, but right or wrong, it was their decision.

"Well Maddie ain't like you can't find a nice man and build a life around these parts. If you fix yourself up some and stop putting all that grease on your face, you could catch the widower Wilbert Truce."

Madelyn frowned. "Mama, please. I ain't got no time to worry about how I look. All I do is work and come home to more work. Wilbert may like me, but I don't care about him with his old self."

"So you say. Remember, Wilbert got his own. He's established, got a big home, a nice one I might add, got his own business, and he's sweet on you. So what he's a bit older? You thirty-years-old, Maddie. Don't you want to get married and have a family 'fore it's too late?"

"A family with Wilbert, Mama? Please stop talking about him. He's not my type, anyway."

"What do you know about your type?" Ophelia laughed. "You act like Wilbert is a hundred years old. He's only in his forties and you need to give him a chance. He ain't interested in those single women from church who chase him around town, especially that Savannah Moses. She ain't right upstairs if you ask me. Anyway, Wilbert only got eyes for you. Plus, he's a nice looking, dark skin man. Reminds me of your daddy. And those eyes…" Ophelia smiled in remembrance. "You stubborn like that man was, girl. Don't miss out on a good thing!"

SYNOPSIS

Madelyn, the youngest sibling of the Johnson trio has had it with the elder, Georgina and Nola who left Lula, Mississippi five years ago, moving up north to Harlem, New York with a vision of becoming a jazz singing duo. They're more than self-centered, leaving their sister with the huge responsibility of handling the affairs of their deceased grandmother, Estelle, as well as their mother Ophelia. This is causing much stress on the young woman, and she feels that her life will be no more than it is. That is until the widower, Wilbert Truce comes along. An older man, fifteen years her senior, to be exact and Madelyn believes he is surely too old for her to love. But she'll soon find out that love has no boundaries and she and Wilbert will embark on a journey filled with one surprise after the next.

Georgina and Nola return to Lula with a secret. Mother, Ophelia has one too. And then we have Savannah Moses, the daughter of Pastor Hezekiah and First Lady Justine Moses who is going to turn this small town upside down. One Good Thing is an emotional rollercoaster of two families whose need to keep things "private" even within their own households, stirs the pot and it overflows.

About the Days of Pleasure Series
9 Books * All Standalones * No Cliffhangers

10 Days of Pleasure

Some relationships are made in the storm. Real love survives them. Basketball star Dallas Avery has the world in the palm of his hand and a lifetime of happiness or despair within his grasp. For accomplished businesswoman, Alicia Mitchell, love is a double-edged sword wrought with happiness and pain. Business calls the soulmates to Scotland but a new, more treacherous storm is brewing back home. Can their love weather this latest test, or will a crueler fate prevail?

20 Days of Pleasure

NBA star Dallas Avery has one intention when he visits the most romantic city in the world—win Alicia Mitchell by any means necessary. They relish their time as a couple—free to explore their magnetic connection in Paris and savor the array of pleasures they discover as soul mates.

But family, friends, the media, and society at large, have various opinions about their complicated relationship. Will Dallas and Alicia find a way to stay together, or will the many factors working against them shatter their once-in-a-lifetime romance?

30 Days of Pleasure

Every end is supposed to be a beginning. After the death of her husband, Alicia Mitchell set herself up financially to embrace freedom and see the world. Then she met a detour. Until NBA basketball star Dallas Avery wrapped his arms around her, Alicia didn't know what it felt like to be cherished. Now he's drawing her focus and shifting her priorities. And Alicia doesn't mind. However, there's a shadow creeping from the edges of her dating history.

Taric Hasan, a man she considered dating until she experienced his dark side, has emerged. Although she once managed to escape him, Taric isn't done with her. He's intent on ending their relationship on his terms … with her death.

40 Days of Pleasure

The NBA's sexy and most valuable player Dallas Avery meets the beautiful Alicia Mitchell, who has one thing on her mind: leaving. Their attraction is intense, but the timing is off. Dallas is determined to convince Alicia to give their May-December relationship a chance, but when their romantic trip to the Caribbean gets derailed by them being embroiled in a local family's deadly drama, romance gets put on the back burner.

50 Days of Pleasure

When an obsessive fan threatens to derail Basketball Superstar Dallas Avery's relationship with the alluring and independent Alicia Mitchell, a trip to Canada comes at the opportune time. The historic sites and chilly landscapes help to stir the growing connection between the couple.

Then a distressed infant is thrust into their care. The teenage mother and her baby are in danger and only trust Dallas and Alicia to help. With the local mob in pursuit and Dallas and Alicia unable to depend on the police, they must flee the country using a historic mode of escape.

60 Days of Pleasure

Determined to give Alicia Mitchell the love that she longs for, NBA-star Dallas Avery whisks her away on exciting adventures around the world.

Dallas let his heart dictate their journey to Seattle and allows the Emerald City to work its magic on Alicia. Until civil unrest involving the indigenous people collides with a dirty politician's plans to use city funds to cover personal debts. A chance meeting with Yuma, a tribal chief's son, creates an opportunity for Dallas to make a difference for those whose voices have been silenced. When an altercation with the police develops after Dallas and Alicia assist a homeless woman, Yuma's tribe is forced to shift gears and protect the couple.

Can Dallas keep the love of his life safe, and will the civil unrest drive a permanent wedge between them?

70 Days of Pleasure

Dallas Avery and Alicia Mitchell are off to Nashville, Tennessee for business and pleasure. Unfortunately, the past returns to haunt the basketball superstar and puts both in imminent danger.

Conway Ackerman has spent the last five years in prison, charged with aggravated stalking of the athlete early in his career. A bitter man with a sordid past, and a psychotic personality, Ackerman has recently been let out of prison and has set a course that will exact the perfect revenge.

While Dallas is aware of the convict's release, he keeps Alicia in the dark. The stage is set for a myriad of adventures, which will extend to the iconic Beale Street in Memphis, but danger is in the midst. A race against time ensues as the couple is tracked from place to place. Will they survive or meet their demise at the hands of a man whose mental state is deadly?

80 Days of Pleasure

From a romantic picnic in the Southwest to jet-setting around the globe to exotic destinations, Dallas Avery lays the foundation for a long-lasting relationship with Alicia Mitchell, brick by brick, beginning with these five words, "Just one more day, baby."

While traveling the romantic countryside from Munich, Germany to Schloss Neuschwanstein, a case of mistaken identity threatens their freedom and possibly their lives. Dallas has faced numerous threats, but nothing could have prepared him for this experience. A desire to make Alicia's childhood dream come true has evolved into an incredible nightmare.

Dallas and Alicia struggle to learn the new rules of engagement they have been forced to play by. One thing is certain, the NBA player is determined they will not be on the losing end.

90 Days of Pleasure

Alicia Mitchell, is and was, the only woman Dallas Avery has ever loved. He strives to soothe her fears about their age difference, the unresolved issues of her past, and is determined to make her his forever.

An impromptu trip to Durabia brings more danger to their relationship. Crown Prince Amir sets his sights on Alicia and puts a diabolical plan in motion for her to be secretly brought into the palace where he can have her all to himself. None of them could fathom that a third party would intervene, and plunge Dallas and Alicia in the middle of a brotherly war.

USA TODAY Bestselling Author, Naleighna Kai, tells the dynamic love triangle of a chance encounter that lands wealthy NBA star, Dallas Avery, back in the arms of Alicia, the woman of his dreams. A woman he hasn't seen in years. A woman he soon discovers is his fiancée's long-lost aunt!

But Tori, isn't ready to give up all that she's worked for in their relationship, so she makes him a shocking offer—go through with the wedding and she'll still allow him to be with the one woman he now can't seem to do without. Dallas will get a family, something her aunt can't give him and Tori will have the lifestyle she clamors. And Alicia will embrace the love she's longed for all her life and that had already been in her reach before she disappeared. Everyone will get a little of what they want. . . and maybe a whole lot of what they don't.

The details of the trio's love life play out in the tabloids and on talk shows, making Dallas the center of an NBA scandal. Eventually, the doors slam shut on this open marriage in the making and Dallas is forced to make a choice to end the chaos.